AISLING MAGUIRE was born in Dublin in 1958, where she works as a freelance writer and editor. Her short fiction was first published in the 'New Irish Writing' page of the *Irish Press*. Since then her work has appeared in several anthologies, including *Raven Introductions 4* (Raven Arts, 1986), *The Dolmen Book of Short Stories* (Dolmen, 1986), volumes one and two of *The Blackstaff Book of Short Stories* (Blackstaff Press, 1988 and 1991), and *Figures in a Landscape: Writing from Ireland* (Cambridge University Press, 1995). She has contributed book reviews to the *Irish Independent*, the *Irish Times*, the *Sunday Tribune* and RTÉ radio. *Breaking Out* is her first novel.

GW00367396

breaking out
aisling maguire

THE
BLACKSTAFF
PRESS

BELFAST

ACKNOWLEDGEMENT

The author wishes to thank the Tyrone Guthrie Centre, and Joan and Michael Gleeson, for providing space in which to write.

First published in 1996 by Blackstaff Press Limited
with the assistance of
The Arts Council of Northern Ireland
and grant-aided by
An Chomhairle Ealaíon

This edition first published in 2002 by Beeline
an imprint of Blackstaff Press Limited
Wildflower Way, Apollo Road
Belfast BT12 6TA, Northern Ireland

Typeset by Techniset Typesetters, Newton-le-Willows, Merseyside

Printed in Great Britain by Cox & Wyman

A CIP catalogue record for this book
is available from the British Library

ISBN 0-85640-732-1

www.blackstaffpress.com

for my father

Faces bobbed above Eleanor Leyden's cradle.

'Who does she favour?' they asked and laughed at the little fist clenched in rebellious salute.

Margaret, drawing a finger over her infant's cheek, replied, 'She's like herself.'

Yet, at her daughter's call in the trough between moonlight and dawn, she was carried out of sleep by eagerness to hold the scented flesh and measure again the eyelashes, the ridge of the nose, as if in darkness these might have altered. Now and then fear plumbed her chest and she bent to listen for the child's heart. Reassured for the present, her anxiety swung to her daughter's future, which stretched from that high summer of 1960 into the gulf of another century. Overwhelmed, Margaret would collapse, hands stanching tears. Later, she laughed with the mirror at the bulge of her cheeks and her raw eyes, but the worry never ended.

Margaret reneged on the apostasy she had agreed with

Colm, and entrusted their daughter to religion's old security. She hurried towards the church, cursing the downpour as the pram tyres careened through puddles and drops eeled into her collar. In the portico her brother Ray waited, already winged in his white surplice.

'Are they here?' she whispered.

He nodded as they hiked the pram up the steps.

'Oh, the poor child.' The toss of her head spread drops on the air.

'Here, let me do that.' Ray unsnapped the canvas pram cover while his sister dried herself with a hankie. 'She's as warm as toast!'

The baby, raised from the parcel of blankets, nuzzled his vestment.

Greyed in the stone light of the church, Margaret's aunt and uncle drew pride from their vigil at the baptismal font.

'You're doing right,' Uncle Bernard encouraged.

Briefly, Margaret balked at the certainty shepherding her to the brink of the stone basin. Her conscience reproved her faltering loyalty to Colm. She gaped like a fish in air but met only the admonishment of saints trapped in the leaden mesh of stained glass.

'Give me the wean.' Aunt Nuala delved her niece's cradling arms.

The elderly woman's fur coat so embraced the child that Margaret could no longer see her daughter's face. Apart, while all routed Satan and his pomps, Margaret bunched her hands in her pockets, knowing, too late, that it was her own solace she had come for. Her brother, anonymous in the posture of celebrant, fumbled through the white robe to anoint the chest. The infant sent up a high wail as salt grated her tongue and water chilled her downy fontanel.

'Another soldier for Christ.' Nuala's rosy lips quivered on her godchild's forehead before returning her to Margaret.

'Suffer the little children,' Bernard intoned.

Ray sighed, and kissing his stole, unlooped it from his neck. 'Father Deane has the car today. Otherwise I could run you all home,' he apologised.

'Don't worry.' Margaret flashed him a smile. 'We're hardy. Aren't we, Eleanor?' She clasped the sobbing child to her chest, closing her eyes, with an urge to reimplant the small body in her own.

On the steps outside Bernard agitated a large umbrella. 'Would you like us to escort you, dear?'

'No thanks. It was bad enough of me to bring you out on a day like this.'

'No, no.' Bernard shook his head. 'We're glad to do a Christian duty, isn't that so, Nuala?'

'Of course.' Impatience ticked in his wife's features. 'For the love of God, Bernard, give me that umbrella. You'll have it crucified before the day's end.'

'There you are.' He bent towards Margaret. 'She's the brains of the family.'

Margaret pressed a kiss to his jowl. 'You're a good man,' she said.

'Bye-bye, dear.' Nuala punched the umbrella into bloom.

Halted one morning at the ironing board, Margaret calculated that four months had passed since Eleanor's birth. But the days have run so fast, she thought, where to? All melted into my baby.

She moved to bend over the closed face. Strands of red hair lit the infant's skull. 'Goldilocks,' she murmured. 'I am mad with love for you.'

On the windowsill the kitten attended autumn's fling, her head swaying to the aria uncoiling from the radio.

'The whole circle of love,' Margaret aphorised.

As the iron arrowed through creases in Colm's shirts she mapped excursions they would make with their daughter, eager to rediscover the world through innocent eyes.

'When is Ray for Africa?'

'Next Tuesday.' Margaret looked down at her empty plate.

'Is it itchy feet or delusions of sainthood he has?'

'He believes in God.'

'That's his worry.' Colm scraped his chair back. 'He shouldn't go spreading it to total strangers. All he'll get in return is a dose of malaria or leprosy. Then he'll be rightly Albert Schweitzered.'

'What's leprosy?'

'It's when you get so sick that your hands and nose fall off.'

'Don't do that, Colm.'

'You can't wrap her in cotton wool.'

Winded with panic, the child looked to her mother. 'Is that true?'

'In a way. But it doesn't happen here. Only in poor places like Africa.'

'Here you just get cancer and rot.' Colm stood and moved to the window. Planting his hands on the sill, he leaned his forehead against the glass. 'There's strife here too. We're only half a nation.'

'Help me clear the table, Eleanor.' Margaret handed a plate to the child. 'Daddy's in a brown study.'

'Half-baked,' he continued sardonically.

'You can't take on everybody's worries.' Margaret tucked against her husband's side.

Colm's arms draped her shoulders. 'You get the same way too, but you hold it in.'

Pegged between her parents, Eleanor stared over the road and the abandoned gardens tangling down to the railway line.

'Ah, shag it,' Colm whooped, and, raising the sash, stuck out his head to shout, 'Up the Republic!'

His words dissolved in the soft evening. The fog-horn lowed in the channel. Lights sleeved the curve of the bay and spotted Howth's brow. Eleanor inhaled the stillness of pure love.

Two years later that love was shattered.

Colm's borrowed car droned through November dusk. He drove slowly, somnolent after Sunday lunch with friends.

'Are we nearly there?' Eleanor fretted in the back seat.

'Soon,' Margaret said. 'Soon we'll be home. Try to sleep, love.'

But Eleanor was laughing now, looking past her mother at the tractor lights skittering towards them on wet leaves. The bonnet rucked like foil over her parents and she was pitched to the floor, submerged by splintering glass. She tried to call but crystals filled her mouth. Pain bolted her left arm, pushed her to the limits of herself. Across that blackness she heard the wreckage stir and moans brokenly sounding her name; then screams; then silence.

In the months immediately following their deaths, Margaret and Colm persisted like a garment around Eleanor. She looked for them behind the curtain of cascading glass. Power returned to her spastic arm and she was airborne, swinging between her parents like a clapper in a bell. 'More, more, more,' she panted. Laughing, they dropped her in a snowdrift and tumbled after her. Side by side by side they lay, scissoring arms and legs, the snow creaking as it accommodated their effigies. Cold gripped Eleanor's limbs until Margaret, calling 'chillo, chillo, chillo', leapt up and hauled the child out of her snowbed. Light stirred the angels' wings. Eleanor waited to see them flare, and mantling with the fires of sunset, rise like kites to become skyborne extensions of herself and her parents. But they were pinned to the ground.

Margaret's toe scuffed the edge of the smallest angel's wing.

'Don't,' Eleanor screamed. 'Don't.'

'All right,' Colm soothed, 'we'll leave the angels

be. Come on, I'll give you a piggyback.'

'No.' She pouted and stood over the impression in the snow.

When she looked around, her parents had reached the bend in the path. They were watching her. She glanced back at the angels, shadowed now by the darkening January sky. She saw the wings shudder and fail.

'Wait for me.' She panicked, running down the path as her parents stooped to catch her.

Her new home was one of a red Edwardian terrace backing on to the River Dodder. Eleanor, her arm dangling limp at her side, was delivered to her parents' friends, the O'Driscolls, by her Aunt Nuala. Throughout the journey from Crumlin to Ballsbridge she had knelt on the rear seat, fondling a suedette dog couched amid plastic flowers on the back window. His mute bobbing head commiserated with her loneliness.

'Sit down, dear.' Nuala gently pulled the tail of the child's duffel coat.

Eleanor slid away from the old woman.

On the doorstep Nuala refused Angela's offer of tea. 'Now that I have the taxi, I'll go on home. Be good, Child of Grace,' Nuala whispered and approached a powdery cheek to the child.

Angela's hand feathered Eleanor's shoulder as they watched Nuala ease herself into the taxi. 'Wave goodbye,' she prompted.

The small hand flexed, not at tearful Auntie Nuala, but at the joggling toy dog.

Entering the house, Eleanor asked, 'Who is Grace?'

'I don't know,' Angela said. 'Why?'

'Auntie Nuala called me Child of Grace.'

'Some people say that.'

'Why?'

Her new mother exhaled deeply. 'Well, because when you are baptised you enter into a state of grace. It's a gift from God.'

Eleanor was mystified.

'Do you know about God?'

She shook her head.

'I see.' Angela's eyes scanned the air, as if in search of grace. 'I see,' she repeated. 'We'll soon remedy that. Now come upstairs and see your room.'

Her hands engaging the child and the suitcase, Angela climbed the stairs at the six-year-old's deliberate pace.

'That's Ronan's room.' The door was shut and a green plastic paratrooper hung from the door knob. 'And that's our room. So you'll know where to come if you need us in the night.'

Through the framing angle of the open door, Eleanor saw deep red carpet yawn into a bay window draped with red and white floral curtains; the same curtains hung from the kidney dressing table and hid the legs of the bed. Every leak of space was stoppered.

'It's funny.' She giggled.

'We like it.' Angela turned. 'You're up here.'

A short flight of stairs brought them to a room set under the eaves. In the black grate a paper fan stiffened.

'See. You have a view of the garden.' Angela drew the child towards the half-railed window. 'Dermot has some planting to do.'

Desolate borders islanded the lawn. A yellow towel slapped on the clothesline. The river gouged its course behind the rear wall of the terrace. Eleanor shivered, as if she had been licked by the dark water.

'Have you got a boat?'

'Good Lord, no,' Angela laughed. 'That water's filthy.' She wheeled away from the window. 'Why don't we go to the kitchen and have a hot drink? Ronan will be in soon.'

Supporting her good hand on the banisters, Eleanor followed her foster mother down the stairs until Angela's sudden halt checked her.

'Oh, I nearly forgot. There's a loo up there if you want to spend a penny.'

Eleanor shook her head. Although she had not heard the phrase before, she could guess what it meant. Its silliness made her self-conscious.

'Are you sure?' Angela entreated.

She nodded.

As they proceeded, Colm's voice sang in her ear:

Christmas is coming and the geese are getting fat,
Please to put a penny in the poor man's hat.
If you haven't got a penny a halfpenny will do
And if you haven't got a halfpenny then
    Marx will help you.

By the time they reached the kitchen the scald had swollen from her throat and overspilled her cheeks.

'Oh dear, dear, dear.' Angela crouched to draw the child's head into the nook of her shoulder, and hooping her arms, fumbled for a hankie in her sleeve.

Eleanor straightened. 'I'm sorry,' she gulped. 'I . . . I do want to go to the toilet.'

'That's all right, dear.' Angela's tone cleared. 'There's a cloakroom under the stairs.' She guided her back into the hall. 'You might as well get to know the whole house today.' Her laugh strained. 'After all, it's your home now.'

Angela's form rippled over the frosted-glass door panels. Eleanor sat on the closed toilet lid. Swivelling around, she lifted the crocheted top hat from the cistern, worked it off the paper roll and perched it on her head. Mockery accented by a scar on her right eyebrow grinned in the mirror above the hand basin. Doffing towards the door, Eleanor allowed the hat to slip till it landed upside down on the ox-blood tiles. Angela shuddered again behind the glass. Her cough rang in the hall. As best she could, Eleanor scrabbled the roll back into the hat. Then she flushed the toilet and emerged from the cubbyhole.

'Good girl.' Angela sketched a smile. 'Now here's the living room.'

Eleanor was fascinated by her foster brother. She regarded him with the wariness of a foreigner, uncertain how to break into speech with him. She stared at his pudding-bowl haircut and peered into his little porthole glasses. The freckles swarming on his skin made him look scruffy. His breath smelt of eggs. During her first weeks in his house he behaved as though she were invisible.

In the afternoons while Ronan was still at school Eleanor marched around the garden, chanting. A green door broke the wall at the foot of the garden. Lacking a handle, it could lead nowhere. Often she stood, her toe jammed in its gnawn sill, hearing the river's sound flush the warped planks and blistering paint. Through the rusting keyhole she could spy a brief eddy gathering froth and weeds. One day she saw the old door melt into the garden, hauling a surge, until it rose and swilled the ledge of her dormer window and she set sail in her suitcase square-rigged with a billowing sheet.

'What's so funny?' Angela posed her hands on her hips.

Eleanor's titter stopped. She snapped around without replying.

'Will you help me with these clothes?'

She plodded to Angela's side and drew a vest of Dermot's from the basket and held it out.

'Oops. Try not to drop them on the ground, love.' Angela retrieved the dangling shoulders.

Eleanor slipped one of Ronan's socks between her mittened thumb and forefinger.

'I'm sorry that Ronan doesn't play with you,' Angela said. 'But he will. He's not used to a sister. Eight years is a long time on your own.' She jogged her sigh into a laughing tone. 'Soon you'll be as tight as ticks, Dermot says.'

Eleanor tendered a blouse.

'When I was a child I used to pray for a sister. I'd like to have one now.' Angela's voice drifted, then, recollecting herself, she bent towards Eleanor. 'That's why I'm glad to have you,' she said, holding one end of the blouse and shaking it, as if to test the strength of her connection to the child.

Eleanor released the garment and wandered back to the end of the garden.

That night, her eyes hugging the straw of light in the partly open door, Eleanor listened to Dermot having words with his son.

'You must be nicer to Eleanor. You should be glad to have a sister.'

'But Dad, she's a girl,' Ronan whined.

'Sisters usually are. I had great times with your

aunts. They pulled me everywhere in a go-cart.'
Dermot laughed. 'I was like Caesar himself. They
don't like to be reminded of it now, but,' he reflected.
'Anyway, son, I'm not saying you're to do that with
Eleanor. Only be kind to her. Mum says she's lonely
in herself.'

When Ronan admitted the girl to his bedroom he
shared a secret with her. Arms straining around his
bedside locker, he cleared it from the wall. 'There,'
he whispered. 'It's the War Zone.'

Eleanor crouched into the wedge of shadow and
fingered the layers of peeling wallpaper.

Over her shoulder Ronan pointed to land masses
and seas defined by the ragged patterns. 'The king of
the Blue Land is trying to take over the Red Land.'

The girl pulled away a corner of striped paper.
Crumbs of flesh-pink plaster dusted the skirting
boards.

'We can only play at night,' the boy continued, 'so
that Mum doesn't see us.'

'Then I can't play.' Eleanor frowned.

'I'll ask her to let you sleep in here tonight.'

'All right.'

He stretched an imaginary line with his hand. 'You
can have the Red Land.'

'But you have more than me.'

'I was here first.' His eyes widened as he notched his
glasses to the bridge of his nose.

The girl studied the patchy maps and she saw how
the Red Land could be expanded to contain the Blue.

★

Torchlight enlarged the paper world to a palpable landscape, scarred by a rift in the plaster. Week by week the stealthy game continued. Leaning from their beds into the lit space, the children created jungles, rivers, cities, and launched attacks from the sky and the sea. Flakes of paper and plaster littered the floor. Stalemate occurred the day Angela's hoover choked behind the beds. Interrogated, the children flushed and shook their heads, mumbling in their new solidarity. Dermot added his rebuke to his wife's. The following weekend the smell of fresh paint invaded the house as he glossed the damage. Two coats later the Red and Blue Lands were obliterated.

That Christmas Eleanor was given a doll as a playmate. Naming the pert-faced dummy provoked dispute, Dermot favouring Marilyn, Angela suggesting Alice. Eleanor insisted on Margaret.

Ronan christened the doll over a bucket of water. Robed in his dressing gown, with a white towel draped around his neck, he chanted gibberish. 'Say amen,' he directed Eleanor.

'But she's a girl.'

'Everyone says that after their prayers, silly.' He gibbered again. 'Now.'

'A man. Do you hear that Margaret? You're a man.' The plastic eyelids clicked shut.

'What happened to Margaret?' Angela looked at the newly christened but now one-armed doll.

'She wanted to be like me,' Eleanor explained.

'But you have two arms, love.'

The child's right hand cradled the spastic left

against her chest.

'Poor Margaret.'

Eleanor grasped the doll by its hair and threw it at Angela. Blanching, the woman firmed her jaw to forestall the tears already glistering in her eyes. When Angela had left the room Eleanor retrieved the doll and sat rocking it on her knee with a doleful hum.

From time to time Eleanor peeped at the space on Ronan's wall where, scant as a shadow beneath the thick paint, she could see the contours of the world she had made. 'There, Margaret, that was the Red Land.' She pointed her companion at the elusive line. 'They've hidden it, but the war's not finished.'

Eleanor searched in Dermot's sisters for the little girls who had been his slaves. Both older than Dermot, only Maeve with her squat figure and high colour resembled him.

'You must come and visit my girls one day,' she said.

Eleanor shied from the engulfing smile.

Katherine diverged from the family type. In her lofty stride her blond scrolled head seemed to graze the ceiling. Eleanor, straddled on a pouffe, leaned towards her. With a hooting laugh Katherine pronounced herself 'surrounded by men'. She swung towards her husband in whose stern expression she never failed to raise a whimsical flicker.

'My wife boasts,' he said.

'Can you believe it? We're away to Califor-ni-a for Andrew's sabbatical next September.'

'Are you taking the boys?' Angela worried.

'Oh yes. Lock, stock and barrel.'

'Won't they miss a lot in school?'

'Not at all. It'll do them good to see what's on the other side of the fence.'

'My wife means it will satisfy her compulsion to look over the fence.'

'You should come over to us for a holiday.'

A thin laugh shook Angela. 'Where would we get that sort of money?'

'Save, borrow – chance of a lifetime.'

'I'll tell Dermot you said so.'

'Buy him a Sweepstake ticket.'

Katherine winked at Eleanor. Excitement swooped in the child's chest.

As soon as the guests had left, Eleanor turned to Angela. 'Where is Califor-ni-a?'

'A long way away,' Angela sighed.

Reaching towards lamp switches, she brushed back the winter twilight. Light surprised seams of fatigue on her face. 'They say the sun shines all the time.' Angela might have been talking to herself.

'I want to go there.'

'So do I. So do I.'

'If we were birds we could fly.'

'If . . .'

Their glances touched, then deflected. Eleanor twitched on the pouffe, then crossed the room to be smoothed in the scented fold of Angela's embrace. The woman, in turn, drew comfort from the child, her hand rhythmically caressing the small shoulder.

'By the time you're grown up,' she said, 'you'll have your holidays on the moon.'

Eleanor saddened under Angela's distracted kiss.

Under the smile of a golden child in a cinctured robe Eleanor spent her mornings pouring macaroni shells and rice grains from cups to bowls and back again, or learning to count beads on a wire. Her classmates teased her.

'My mummy says you're a orphan,' declared one with moles on her face.

Eleanor plucked at the wire.

Emboldened by her friend, a curly-headed girl approached her. 'Is that why you have a funny arm?'

'I broke it.'

'Did you go to the hospital?' asked another.

'Yes.'

'I think the doctor put your arm on backwards.' The curly-haired girl pulled Eleanor's upturned hand. A chill whipped through her as the spastic limb coiled again.

'You look like a monkey.' She laughed.

'And you smell like one too,' the others joined in. 'You live in the zoo,' they chanted, circling her.

Eleanor's head pounded. The coloured beads blurred on their frame. She swung around, but finding no way out of the circle, doubled over to spew a rope of whitish fluid.

When they mentioned the name of the boy in the picture, the children nodded. Eleanor assumed this habit as quickly as she had tumbled to the signs of morning prayer. Her crayons brightened catechism illustrations until, at the sight of Mary's red dress, Mother Sugrue's finger jabbed the page.

'Our Lady always wears blue. Don't you know that?'

Eleanor stared obstinately into the nun's verdigrised teeth.

'You'll come with me, so, at break time to see her in the chapel.'

While her companions sipped their half-pints of milk, Eleanor, her hand clasped in the nun's bony knuckles, was marched along corridors and up flights of stairs. Lavender wax sealed the silence of the wood-panelled chapel. In the choir stalls a solitary nun fondled her rosary.

'Did no one teach you to genuflect?' Mother Sugrue hissed.

Eleanor's head swung.

'Get down on your knee.'

The child knelt.

'One knee.' The nun tugged her arm, grazing the young cheek with her dark serge sleeve.

'Always do that when you enter God's house. Do you hear me?'

Eleanor nodded.

'What do you say?'

'Yes, Mother Sugrue.'

'That's better.'

At a side altar she was made to kneel face to face with a plaster serpent whose maw arched over an apple.

'Look at her dress,' the nun ordered.

Tilting her head back, Eleanor ran her eye up the moulded blue folds to a face tempered by an anxious smile.

'Remember this: blue is Mary's colour. Now we'll light a candle for all the sinners.'

Mother Sugrue released the child's hand and took a night light from the box before the altar, tipped it to one already lit, and set its flame to magnify inside a red plastic cup.

'Now, tell her you're sorry for putting her in scarlet.'

Eleanor turned from the statue to the nun. 'But she's not real.'

The nun's face purpled. Swiftly, before she could withdraw it, Eleanor's hand was seized and smacked, the echoed report startling the old nun in the choir stalls.

'Say after me: *mea culpa, mea culpa, mea maxima culpa.*' Mother Sugrue knelt and thumped her chest.

Hand smarting, Eleanor knocked lightly above her own heart.

'I am truly sorry, Mary, for having offended thee,' the nun added.

Eleanor followed suit, her eyes fixed on the

punctured apple.

Outside the chapel they paused before another statue. 'The *pietà*,' said the nun. 'Our Lady mourns the death of her only son.' Her grip crushed Eleanor's hand. 'You've no right to be adding to her sorrows.'

On the dead man's chest Eleanor saw a wound gape like an eye. 'Who shot him?' she asked.

Mother Sugrue's face quivered her wimple. 'You are a wicked little girl.'

Eleanor flinched, but even through her confusion, defied the nun's contempt.

Told that she was on the threshold of reason, Eleanor heard the word bread translated to Holy Communion. Boasts of Limerick lace and white patent shoes flurried around her. Late one night she followed the murmur of her foster parents' and her uncle's voices to the return landing.

'The child had never been inside a church,' Angela was saying, 'let alone a school.'

'A little heathen,' Dermot added. 'How long did they think they could go on with that home-grown education?'

Resignation weighed in Ray's sigh. 'Well, you know how Colm was set against religion.'

'It's not right to deprive a child of faith. She can reject it later –'

'But Colm maintained the damage was done in the early years,' Dermot put in.

'He left the church. It didn't bother him,' Angela persisted.

'It did. He said he wanted to dip his mind in an acid

bath to clean off the conformist patterns.'

'Children don't like to be different. That's why we had her baptised.'

'But I had baptised her already,' Ray said.

'What?' Angela's voice stretched.

'Margaret wanted it as a safeguard for her own doubts, I suppose.'

A hand–slap cracked the air. 'So she's twice as holy as the rest of us.' Dermot laughed.

'And who were the godparents?'

'Our Aunt Nuala and Uncle Bernard.'

'The silly woman never told me.'

'She was asked to keep it to herself.'

'Still, you'd think after what happened –' Angela quavered. 'Poor Margaret.'

On the morning of Eleanor's First Communion, Ray gave her a rosary made with dried beans the colour of blood: 'The women in my village make them.' Nicotined fingers sifted the beads into her hand.

'But they're heathens,' Ronan said.

'Well' – Ray smiled – 'they're nice people for all that. Anyway, by the time I'm finished they'll have found God – I hope. If we are allowed to stay after independence.'

'Do you have leprosy?' Eleanor quizzed her uncle.

'Only heathens get leprosy, silly,' Ronan said.

Sudden tears rushing her face, Eleanor sprang from the sofa and ran into the hall.

'Eleanor!' Midway up the stairs, Ray caught her, and sitting on the step, circled her waist with his arm.

'Here, blow.' He pressed a hankie to her nose. 'Better?'

She shook her head.

'What's wrong? Tell me.'

She retched big sobs. 'I have leprosy.'

'Nonsense.' He laughed. 'How do you make that out?'

She held up her twisted arm.

'That's not leprosy. It's . . . it's broken. That's all.'

'Dermot said I was a heathen.'

'He was teasing.' Ray smoothed her hair. 'Look at you all dressed up for your First Communion. Jesus will enter your heart today, the way a bird sits on a nest. And He'll stay as long as you want Him. Now: dry your eyes and put on a smile for Him.'

Cold air streamed down Eleanor's side. The white dress and net veil estranged her from herself and she flinched as her father's dry laugh stung her ear.

'Jesus is your friend,' Ray said. 'He will watch you as He watches all of us.'

Eleanor drew back from her uncle. His pale eyes looked away from her. She looked down at the stranger's neat white shoes and frilly socks. Even her fingers were about to be swallowed by lacy gloves. Disconnection dizzied her.

'Here's Ronan now.' Ray chucked her under the chin. 'Show him how brave you are.'

Fist gouging her eyes, she licked the salt from her lips and made space for Ronan to squeeze in beside her. She warmed in the pressure of his body and his familiar smell.

'That's for you.' He blushed, dropping a package

into her lap.

Slowly she unravelled the green paratrooper that had guarded his door. She snivelled and laughed.

'Come on, let's watch him fly.'

The children craned over the banisters as the plastic soldier dallied down the air to the hall table.

California had expanded Katherine. Ever since her return, her hooting laugh reverberated a deeper bass and her conversation curved invariably to the arguments trembling the air of the west coast.

'Only for this war I'd happily live there,' she told Dermot. 'But I wouldn't like to see my boys conscripted.'

'If everyone said that during the last war, where would we be now?'

'Better off, maybe.'

'You're being naïve.'

'There are plenty who think like me. You're too insular, Dermot, and it shows in your newspaper. You should have visited us out there.'

'So be it.' Dermot pushed out of his chair. 'I only hope Andrew hasn't lost the use of his reason, too.'

'He's more sensitive than you are. He cried when the brother of one of his students was killed. They shipped home all the bits in a plastic bag. The parents don't even know if it was their own son they buried.'

'For Christ's sake, Katherine, I'm not a stone. But you can't weigh every corpse against the issue.'

'Issues are only feathers compared to a human life.'

'Human lives make the issues. What about the Vietnamese? What about the way they're suffering under the communists?'

'The Americans are no better. It's imperialism in both cases.'

'Ha. You're brainwashed, girl, and no mistake.'

'Don't patronise me, little brother.' Katherine strode from the room and the front door clinched.

'I can't understand it. She's an intelligent woman.' Dermot scowled.

Outside the window leaves flaked from the grey sky.

'I wouldn't like Ronan to go to war,' Angela ventured, 'especially one he didn't understand.'

'Now don't you start,' Dermot said. 'If Katherine goes on with this nonsense, she'll not be welcome here.'

Angela firmed her lips against protest.

'Give it a rest. I expect peace and sanity when I come home.'

Raising her head from her copybook, Eleanor watched the stoop of Angela's back as she worked at the sink.

'Why did Dermot make you stop talking?'

'That's a funny question.' Angela turned to face her.

'You let Dermot win.'

'It's nothing to do with winning or losing.' Angela

spread her hands, flinging soap suds across the floor. 'You have to keep a balance in a relationship, in a marriage.'

'I think Dermot's mean to you and to Katherine.'

'No, love,' Angela said. 'It's complicated.'

The child stared into the woman's self-doubt.

'Finish your sums,' Angela said, and returned to the dishes.

Eleanor's pencil scrawled a huge X over the copy-book. 'I hate sums,' she said.

'I hate washing dishes,' Angela said, 'but they've got to be done.'

Katherine's sons also exhaled a frank new confidence. Their manner had broadened with their syllables and Tom, the eldest, shooting towards adolescence, ditched old-world deference to greet his uncle and aunt as equals. Behindhands, Eleanor and Ronan were told that their cousin had learnt to drive. He scoffed at his mother's new Mini Minor and, one bright August, as the car nosed through sunlit clearings and pools of shade on the road to the family caravan at Silver Strand, he mimed the interplay of pedals and gears. Later, drawling the word to emphasise the length of the auto, he traced his Mustang dream in the hard sand of the shore.

To match the boys, Eleanor shrugged away her deformity. Abreast with them in the waves, she plunged towards the sandbank; like a bolt of cloth un-furling, she pitched herself down the dunes and it was she who persuaded Tom to pinch the speedboat parked on the strand. Paul, the baby, was sandwiched between her and Ronan in the back as, under Michael's navigation, Tom throttled the engine and pushed it into gear, then bounced the bow over the waves. A dog on the shore volleyed barks at the motor's roar and chased along the tide line. Eleanor's laughter whooped; Ronan giggled, protectively splaying his hands over his glasses. Elated by the release of power, Tom leaned back, singing riffs of 'Surfin' USA'. Michael, in the same pose, struck an accompanying bongo on the dash. Tom spun the wheel and the boat slalomed over the swell. Spray flew up, smarting the children's eyes, whetting their lips.

'Yo ho ho and a bottle of rum,' Michael yelled.

Paul screamed in terror as Tom pushed it up to full power and the bow sprang off the water. Freedom panted in Eleanor's chest. The buzz of the engine ripped through her limbs. Turning, she saw the shore fade to indeterminate bands of colour. The boat's keel tore up the surface of the water. Suddenly, the engine died. The bow smacked onto the waves.

'Shit!' Tom hit the petrol gauge. 'Out of gas.'

'There's got to be a spare tank somewhere,' Michael said.

Their voices sounded hollow. The grinding wake slackened, its foam sliding into the sea.

'I want my mummy,' Paul wailed.

A chill stole through Eleanor's numbed arm.

'Maybe there's oars.' Ronan's tone was tinged with panic. He and Michael rummaged under the seats while Tom tinkered with the ignition. Over and over the engine chugged and died.

'No go.' Tom shrugged.

'Fuck.' Michael kicked the gunwale. 'It's your fault,' he rounded on Eleanor.

'I don't care,' she said. 'I hope we float to America.'

'Noooo.' Paul's protest echoed like the call of a strange bird.

'Leave her alone,' Tom said. 'It was all our faults. Anyway, they'll send out a lifeboat. We just have to sit and wait.'

Time stopped as the boat idled between two horizons.

'I'm hungry.' Ronan rubbed his stomach.

'Then catch a fish,' Tom snorted and pulled a soggy packet of cigarettes out of his shirt pocket.

Michael and Ronan stood at the stern, waving and calling for help until they were hoarse.

Worming her way into the bow, Eleanor crouched beside Tom.

'Can I have a pull?' she asked.

He passed her the cigarette and she sucked hard. The smoke gagged her throat and scorched her eyes.

'Breathe, don't suck,' Tom said.

She tried again, this time letting the smoke take root in her lungs. 'That's nice.' She handed back the cigarette. 'I like it here. It's peaceful.' She closed her eyes, yielding to the loll of the boat and the pumped-up sensation in her chest.

Ronan and Michael had given up their SOS and leaned over the gunwale, dabbling the water, snatching at ribbons of seaweed. Paul's whimpering shuddered into hiccups.

Tom launched smoke rings above their heads. 'Smoke signals.' He nudged Eleanor.

'Show me.' Her efforts corkscrewed and stumbled against his.

'Gently, gently,' he encouraged, his finger pulsing against her cheek until her breathing dropped into a new rhythm and a perfect circle floated clear of her puckered mouth.

'Again, again,' she begged, but the cigarettes were finished.

Tom tossed the empty pack into the water and pointed to where the rescue boat was blundering out from the shore.

'Aaw.' Eleanor shrank into the corner of her seat, elation shrivelling.

After that day Eleanor stayed close to Tom. Beside him at table she noticed the hair fringing his upper lip, curious to touch it. When everyone, including Katherine, had gone to bed she stayed up to gamble her last broken matches against his in 'one more – one more – just one more' game of pontoon.

Paul and Ronan sniggered. 'Nelly's in love with Tom.'

Eleanor's petulant kicking battered their tease to yelps, until Tom hooked her under the arms and swung her away.

'You're like a boy,' he said, planting her on the sand.

She braced to attention. 'Good.'

Taking a last-day look, Eleanor and Tom walked the beach. Indigo clouds queered the light on the dunes. At the crest of one mound Tom halted and screwed his fingers into a telescope.

'If you could see far enough,' he speculated, 'you would see to the end of our universe and into the next one.'

'What's in there?' Eleanor's short fingers whorled to a keyhole of blue.

'The same as here. And the two of us standing on a sand dune watching ourselves.'

'It's a mirror, then?'

'Yes. Except that we can't see our reflection.'

'How do you know it's there?'

'I don't, but I have a hunch.' His fist unrolled.

Eleanor kept hers funnelled, pins and needles charging her skin. She knew that hunch. Tired of pushing for a glimpse of that world where another version of herself lived, she looked down to see Tom pressing his forefinger to a spear of marram grass, quivering it there till blood fruited on his skin.

'Lick it,' he commanded.

She wrinkled her nose at the red globe which swelled and teetered with the weight of its own life.

'Go on,' he urged. 'It won't kill you.'

She shut her eyes and dabbed the red drop. Reluctant to swallow it, she let its tang soak into her tongue.

'Chickens run around when their heads are cut off and blood keeps coming out like a fountain,' he said slyly. 'They don't know they're dead.'

'I don't believe you.'

'You have to,' he said, 'or else I'll tell everyone you're a bloodsucker.' He laughed, then suddenly knelt up, head attent.

Eleanor crept to his side. A tremulous male voice

frisked through the dunes. The children climbed to the summit and spied in the canyon a chrome antenna probing space. Next to the transistor a man lay over a woman. Her fingers clutched his back, pulling at his shirt. Above them the lone voice cantered. The woman's light dress furled at her hips where the man's pelvis bobbed. Beneath his nuzzling face her lacquered head swooned on a soft cardigan. The commentator's voice screeched urgently, rounding bends, panting towards the post. Eleanor pressed her giggles into the back of her hand and glanced at Tom. His faint moustache was emphasised by a blush. He did not return her look even when she backed away. She waited at the foot of the dune but he strode by. She plodded behind him until he paused.

'Stop following me.' He scowled.

Eleanor watched him recede. The radio jabber was slowing down. She turned, imagining the bodies unfastening, and ran off at a tangent to Tom's steps. Pent-up thunder distilled the air. She fretted and wheeled about, seeing the dunes repeat ceaselessly around her, feeling her world waver in a new and terrifying direction. She felt the strangers following her. She would not look back.

Tom's silhouette sprouted on the crest of a dune. She hailed him and stumbled upwards, but he ignored her and proceeded to walk, hands in his pockets, a tuneless whistle seething on his lips. One by one, tepid raindrops broke around them.

'Wait for me,' she called.

He hesitated while she approached, then walked on.

'What were they doing, Tom?' she panted.

'Nothing.' He resumed his whistling.

She started at the sight of their long shadows, fearing that the strangers had caught up with them. She looked back but the dunes had vanished behind the loosening sheets of rain.

Every week Eleanor's grandmother touched the child's face and the girl in turn shut her eyes to dabble the old woman's cheeks with her fingertips.

'Counting my wrinkles?' Gran asked the enquiring fingers.

Eleanor withdrew her hand and set it to read her own features. 'Even if you had big eyes, Gran,' she said, 'you wouldn't be able to see me.'

'Maybe not. But I can see through you, all right.'

'Who will I be when I grow up?' Eleanor puzzled.

'Yourself. Who else?'

'But my name is the same as yours.'

'Don't worry. You'll be you.'

'Then who will you be?'

'I'll be me. A name is only like a label you stick on a pot of jam. The important thing is what's inside.'

'Oh.' For an instant Eleanor felt a part of herself come adrift, as bark cracks from a tree.

'And the worst sin is wanting to be someone else.'

★

Instead of photographs the old woman kept a box filled with mementoes of her family. The cluster of objects swaddled in brown velvet exhaled a faint must. Eleanor unwrapped them one by one and laid them in her grandmother's hands, warming to the lives they conjured.

Her great-grandmother bowed over the missal whose bone-coloured pages were almost transparent.

'She was very devout,' Gran said. 'She never disputed God's will. Neighbours brought relics and cures but she wanted none of them. Not when I lost my sight, not when my brother Colm that your father was named for, came home from the civil war with that bullet in his leg.'

Eleanor rolled the shell in her hand and poked it into her leg, testing for her granduncle's incredulous pain.

'Were you cross with her?'

'Yes. Until one day Colm brought me to a holy well. I mind yet the sting of the water.' She laughed. 'Afterwards I felt so guilty and I thought we could never be cured for going behind her back.'

Eleanor's favourite token was the tendril of her father's hair, fiery as her own, tied in a pale blue ribbon. She fondled and combed the hair, as if it breathed in her fingers. Peeping at her grandmother, she pulled a strand from the bow before replacing it in the box.

Gran touched the lock and smiled. 'You should put yours in a locket.'

Eleanor fidgeted. 'I'm going to put it under my pillow. For my dreams.'

When she placed the two halves of a thrush's egg-shell on her grandmother's palm, the old woman shut her eyes.

'Your grandfather courted me with such things: a crispy autumn leaf or a snaggle of sheep's wool off a fence. He was that romantic.' Her face opened in a fond laugh. 'I was waiting every day for him to come in with a mountain on his back!'

'Where is he now?'

'In heaven with your ma and da.'

'Will he come back with them?'

'They'll not be back, alanna.'

Eleanor pouted and twisted the strand of hair around her finger until the palp whitened for want of blood.

'But they said so.'

'It was a dream you were having. Some day we will join them.' The old woman smiled. 'I'll be with them before you. I'll maybe even see them.'

Eleanor glared each morning at the soil in her flowerpot until the first green hyacinth shoot pricked its surface. She wanted to see the movement of growth. Waking in night's blackest hour, her eyes stung with tears, she listened for the soft disturbance of the soil or the slow outstretch of leaf and bloom. At dawn, while light bundled shadow into corners, the process evaded her sight but she felt its pressure like an electric charge on the air. She measured the advance of her solitary stem against that of the serried spears in her grandmother's basin and clapped triumphantly when hers was the first to flourish its white foam.

Angela sniffed the air in Eleanor's bedroom. 'That plant will have to go.'

'No. It's mine.' She ran to the windowsill.

'It'll soak up all the oxygen.'

She frowned. 'I don't want any oxy ... oxy ... oxy.'

'But lovey, you need it to live.'

'No.' The small foot thudded.

'Eleanor. We'll have no bad temper, please.' Angela's expression hardened with emphasis. 'I'm only saying that you have to transplant it. It'll do better in the garden, anyway, and you'll be able to see it from the window.'

'No.' She shook her head and caged the lather of blossom with her fingers. 'I'll give it to Colm and Margaret.'

The next day Eleanor settled into the rear seat of Dermot's car, trowel and fork in her hand, the clay pot clamped between her knees. At the cemetery Ronan wriggled into his father's vacant seat to play the knobs and levers on the dashboard while Dermot, hand pressed to her back, guided Eleanor through the gravelled aisles to the headstone recalling Colm and Margaret Leyden. Their daughter knelt on a piece of cardboard, provided by Angela, and scrabbled at the corner of the plot, dislodging worms and grass and weeds. Dermot moved away. In her island of quiet, Eleanor worked slowly to lever up a wedge of earth until she had formed an exact crater. Before plugging this with her plant, she doubled over the moist gap, and inhaling its wet mineral smell, pressed her face into the hole.

'Take me home,' she ached. 'Take me home.'

The noise of hurrying feet approached. Dermot's hands gripped her shoulders and drew her back onto her hunkers. Wrapping one arm across her chest, he fumbled with his free hand to find a hankie.

'You're all right, you're all right,' he murmured into her hair as he wiped her mud-streaked face.

Eleanor squirmed and strained away, reached for the plant, then calmly set the cone of soil into the hole and patted the grassy mat over the broken ground. When she stood, Dermot tapped her shoulder, as though she had dropped something.

'Aren't you going to say a prayer?'

Eleanor shook her head and turned away from the plot.

Her foster father made the sign of the cross and bowed his head for a few moments.

That night Eleanor stood at her bedroom window, and shrouded by the curtain, pressed her head against the glass. A full moon spread milky vapour on the air and she pictured an answering gleam from her hyacinth's incandescent petals showing a path through the dark.

Unless the Deerview Lodge was full, Syl Tighe, Angela's father, slept in a guest room. His wife slept in the family annexe overlooking a yard where stray potato peels dissolved into tarmac under the tyres of beat-up cars. Eleanor and Ronan spent a fortnight here every summer while their parents grilled under the Spanish sun. Despite the hotel's location in a wooded valley thirty miles from the city, the children were not woken by the chirrup of birds but by the percussion of iron lungs bumping off and onto brewers' lorries. They spent their morning sorting empty bottles in the yard or helping their grandfather in the garden, Ronan driving a hand mower up and down the lawn, Eleanor following to collect the wet, sweet cuttings.

Afternoons were free time for the children. When the glass door had shuddered behind the last guest to go in search of deer, the hotel was becalmed in post-lunch torpor. Kitchen odours staled down gravy-dark corridors; in the lounge a few grey heads lolled and newspapers slipped to the floor. In her office Mrs Tighe nodded over spiked dockets, a cold teapot at her elbow. Eleanor kept watch as Ronan ducked behind the front desk and lifted a handful of keys from their numbered hooks. Together, the children flitted along landings to broach the guest rooms.

Locked in, they bounced on the beds and rifled wardrobes and suitcases, becoming 'guests'. They swaggered in an assortment of mothballed clothes and painted one another's faces with goatees, beauty spots, bold crimson mouths, laughing at the clowns in the mirror.

'Hello, Mr Eleanor.'

'Good day, Miss Ronan.'

They dropped in a frenzy of giggles onto the bed. But their travels were interrupted one afternoon by the sound of voices on the stairs. Leaping up, they tugged off their costumes, stamping and dancing on the clothes as if they were on fire, and scarpered.

That evening, brushing aside their hosts' conciliatory pleas, the offended guests swung their luggage into their car and pulled away from the hotel, the wife's head set in a bulldoggish scowl.

Mrs Tighe scowled, too, when the children stood before her. She poured a preparatory swig from the teapot and followed that by sucking on a peppermint.

'Your parents will be very disappointed,' she began.

Ronan whimpered. 'Ooh, please don't tell them, Nanna. Please, please.'

'This is very serious.' She turned to Eleanor. 'Have you nothing to say for yourself?'

'It was a game,' the girl said indifferently.

'It was badness,' Mrs Tighe shrilled.

'We're not apples.'

'Don't you dare give me cheek, miss. From now on both of you will help the girls clean the rooms and do the wash-up.'

'Sorry, Nanna.' Ronan snuffled.

Eleanor turned to follow him out of the room but Mrs Tighe called her back.

'I warned my daughter,' she said, 'that she was taking on too much. Trouble, I said.'

Eleanor's eye strayed to the teapot.

'Look at me. Trouble,' she continued. 'Don't think that because we're not your natural family you can dance rings around us. You have no right to hurt us. You're not good enough to —'

Eleanor's mute contempt forestalled Mrs Tighe's abuse.

'You should be down on your bended knees every day, thanking God you're not in an orphanage.'

A cry of shame and affront gathered in Eleanor's throat. She clenched herself against it and stared through the woman's sneer.

Later, from the annexe window, Eleanor watched Betty the cook slouch down the drive, arms wrapped around her waist, straining the shoulders of her out-grown coat. She opened the window, wanting to call out to her to run, run away from this mean place. Instead she drew back her arm and lobbed the single pearl earring which had remained clamped to her ear as she fled the bedroom. It spun lustrous in the darkening day to land in the yard.

Schoolmates relished the mystique of Eleanor's orphanhood. When Maureen Lucey clasped Eleanor's shoulder the nuns swatted the back of her hands with a ruler. Maureen pressed her friendship with home-made cakes and Tupperware beakers full of lemon barley. On Saturdays she invited Eleanor to play at her house.

From the Luceys' kitchen wall Queen Elizabeth II, robed in white gown and blue sash, deigned a smile. Nappies steaming on wooden bars above the Aga thickened air already cloyed with stewed oranges. For Eleanor's benefit, Maureen quavered 'God Save the Queen', her English mother's deeper voice lilting proudly into line. For ever in Eleanor's mind those triumphal words were infused with the thrifty industry of Mrs Lucey's kitchen and the taste of golden syrup on milk pan doorsteps.

'We don't need a queen,' she boasted, quoting Dermot. 'We told the English kings and queens to stay at home.'

Maureen's ponderous eyes appealed to her mother.

'That may be,' Mrs Lucey conceded, 'but you have Mr de Valera instead.'

'He's not a king. He's a president.'

'He acts like a king.'

Eleanor chewed her lip and when her hostess had turned away, stuck out her tongue at the stern face on the wall.

In the garden Maureen showed her a piebald rabbit named Smudge, the animal's pink eyes provoking vicarious tears in Eleanor. Maureen stuck a cabbage leaf through a flap in his grille.

'That's his postbox.' She giggled.

The creature ignored his mail.

'Isn't he hungry?' Eleanor poked her finger through the wire.

'He'll eat it when we go away,' Maureen said. 'Come on, I'll show you the greenhouse.'

Eleanor dawdled after her hostess, turning every now and then to see if the rabbit was eating his cabbage leaf. Maureen waved at her from the greenhouse, her round face bobbing above the tomato canes. Breasting the swelter, Eleanor admired the trussed green fruits cupped in Maureen's hand, then stabbed one with her finger and watched its seeds drip to the ground.

'Don't do that!' Maureen cried. 'Daddy will kill us.'

'How will he kill us?' Eleanor jeered, stabbing the second fruit.

Maureen seized Eleanor's good hand, challenge sharpening in her eyes. Eleanor tugged but Maureen's grip burnt her skin. Maureen snickered. Her victim hunched, firming her jaw. Maureen dropped the broken tomatoes and wiped the ooze from her hand onto Eleanor's shorts, but she kicked her, forcing Maureen to capitulate and release her arm.

'Let's play pygmies,' Eleanor suggested.

'What's that?'

'Jungle men.'

Maureen's face puckered.

'Here.' Eleanor snatched a cane from the soil, capsizing one of the tomato plants. 'That's your spear,' she said and pulled another for herself. 'Now we have to paint our faces.' Filling her crooked palm with earth, she licked the forefinger of her right hand, dipped it in the muck, and traced lines over her companion's brow and cheeks. 'You do mine,' she said, proffering the handful of clay to Maureen.

They were disturbed by wails from the younger Luceys, who stood around the rabbit's hutch. Nicky, next in age to Maureen, stepped towards the cage but sprang back with a yelp. The three little ones wailed again, then shrieked as Eleanor and Maureen rushed from the greenhouse brandishing their spears.

'Shut up. It's only us,' hissed Maureen.

'Look at Smudge.' The smallest girl pointed to the hutch.

The rabbit dangled, his head wedged in the feeding flap.

'He tried to bite me when I went to help him.' Nicky sobbed.

The rigid body spasmed against the wire mesh. Eyes aghast, the animal implored the children. Urine singed his white fur and flew in obscene spurts when the body whacked the cage. The children cowered.

Laying her bamboo on the grass, Eleanor walked up to the cage, her hand whipped out to muzzle the creature and ram his head back through the flap. As the children cheered, she unsnibbed the catch on the door and bundled Smudge out of the hutch. Stunned for an instant, he crouched on the lawn, and a moment later sprang down the garden and through the hedge to an adjoining field. The children tumbled after him, uselessly. Eleanor smiled at Maureen, but a sob plucked the girl's lips.

'What did you do that for?' Nicky shouted. 'Now he's gone and we'll never see him again.'

'He wanted to get out,' Eleanor protested. 'It's horrible in there' – she gestured towards the hutch – 'how would you like it?'

'I hate you,' Maureen whined, tears dissolving her war paint. 'You and your stupid games,' she added, watching the muck weep from her chin. 'Mummy,' she bawled and ran towards the house.

Nicky glared at Eleanor before stumping after his brothers and sisters, who continued to call their pet through the privet at the foot of the garden.

'I don't understand you,' Angela said, worried.

Eleanor counted the lampposts flickering by.

'Do you hear me, Eleanor?'

The child was silent.

'Why do such a thing? It was very cruel.'

'They were cruel – keeping Smudge in a box.'

'That was none of your business. He was their rabbit.'

'I don't care.'

'That's just it. You don't care about anyone. I think you are afraid to be nice to people because you don't want them to pity you.'

The lampposts wobbled. Eleanor closed her eyes and held her breath, letting darkness swell inside her.

'You can't shut people out for ever. Remember that.'

Within a week Smudge's flayed carcass was found on a neighbour's lawn, where magpies feasted on the warm entrails. At school Maureen warned her classmates to shun the 'murderer'.

'Are you proud of yourself?' Dermot asked her that night. 'What harm did the Luceys do to you? Or the poor bunny, for that matter?'

Eleanor jumped from her seat. 'I didn't mean to kill Smudge. I only wanted him to escape from stupid Maureen Lucey.' She fled the room, slamming the door behind her.

When Angela came to her bedside with a cup of hot milk and honey, Eleanor was lying awake, her face reflecting the pallid light from the uncovered window.

'Do you want to apologise?' Angela sat next to the child.

Eleanor shook her head.

'It's not good to go to sleep in a temper. Sit up and drink some of this.'

Eleanor looked from the mug to the window, where the moon hung, barred with clouds.

Angela rose and shut the curtains. 'You know you

have to say sorry to Maureen, don't you?'

'I think Smudge wanted to die.'

'Oh no, no, no.' Adult certainty warmed Angela's voice. 'No one wants to die.' Her fingers straightened the bedclothes. 'Now drink your milk and go to sleep.'

Blowing over the cup, Eleanor raised it to her lips, then fell back onto the pillow.

'Good girl.'

When Angela's footfall had ceased, Eleanor slid out of bed and carried the mug to the window. She pulled back the curtains, dropped the sash and spattered the milk on the moonshot darkness.

'That's for you, Smudge,' she whispered.

By the smooth legs tapering from the buckskin knickers, Eleanor knew that Dick Whittington was a woman. Her eyes raked the rapt happy faces lining the stalls to her right and left before she tugged at Angela's sleeve and declared aloud, 'She's not a man.'

'Sssshh!' Angela hissed.

Ronan leaned across his mother's lap to giggle, 'I can see her BTM.'

'Stop it, both of you,' Angela admonished the children.

The man in front of them twisted around reproachfully. Eleanor put out her tongue, then gave her attention to the stage, where a woman was transformed by a confident strut.

That night Eleanor lifted the black scissors from the kitchen hook, stood on a stool before the bathroom mirror, and pouring her hair over her head, sawed with the old blades till her eyes burnt and the red locks strewed the basin like spillikins.

On her first morning at school after the Christmas holiday a strange nun pinched Eleanor out of the chapel file.

'Who did that to your hair?'

'I did.'

'What possessed you?'

Eleanor arched to smirk into her inquisitor's eye. 'I'm going to be a boy.'

'Eleanor, Eleanor,' the nun lamented. 'The Lord made you a woman for his own purposes.'

'How do you know?' She braced herself for a smack.

Instead, the nun's hand clasped hers to lead her away from her companions. For a moment Eleanor feared that she was being drawn irretrievably into the dark community corridors which this nun inhabited.

Stepping into a window bay as if it were a confessional, the nun bent towards Eleanor. 'We all know, dear, how much you miss your mummy and daddy.'

Eleanor felt a sob bubble in her throat but she pushed it back, denying the nun that victory.

'They are with God now,' she continued. 'If you are ever sad or worried you can talk to them through God.'

'He's a trillion zillion miles away and I can't see Him.'

'You must believe in Him.'

'Why?'

'Because without Him life is a lonely business.'

Eleanor looked up at the nun's pale face raddled by broken veins, and for the first time she realised that there might be a human being under the layers of dusty serge. She tried to imagine the nun's nakedness. Her only measure was the one glimpse of Angela's body, accidentally exposed by the split in her dressing gown. The bush of hair between her foster mother's legs was the thing which had most surprised Eleanor; she had wanted to sink her fingers into the dense black curls so like the wool on a toy animal. Angela, seeing her interest, snapped the gown shut like a curtain.

'Do you have a hairy molly between your legs?' she asked the nun.

A blush scorched the wimpled face and the mouth groped for words. 'Don't be impertinent.'

Eleanor perked her head quizzically at the nun. She saw a cold white form, heavy breasts flaccid on the ribs, buttocks hard, a body to be evaded.

'Go back to your class, child,' the nun said quietly.

As Eleanor dawdled down the passage the nun called after her: 'Pray to our Holy Mother for the grace to follow her example.'

Three weeks later a new pupil paraded between the wooden desks, her dark features simpering with disdain. Trailing a rosy musk, Louise Makarios had already emerged from the shell of childhood, and struck wonder in her ten-year-old peers. Instead of the regulation muslin veils worn by them in the chapel, she laid a round of white lace on her head and walked as though she bore a crown.

'I bet it's a paper doily.' Eleanor's neighbour nudged her and the two girls tittered behind their prayer books.

Eleanor fell in love with the jet hair and lozenge eyes, endowed by Louise's Greek father. She envied the fingers which worked like deft animals to braid or knot her hair for gym class, and longed to touch the lustrous skin.

At break time Maureen Lucey assembled her cronies around the stranger, sweetening her favour with sherbet fizz and pineapple chunks. Exiled from that circle, Eleanor sipped her milk alone at her desk, sensing the sly tremor of a shift in her world. Antagonism flickered in the hobnobbing whispers and the new girl whinnied, pointing at Eleanor.

'Look at her hair,' she exclaimed. 'She's like a rooster!' Her queer accent strained the words to a crescendo. 'Cockadoodledooo!' she crowed, flapping her elbows.

'Cockadoodledoo, cockadoodledoo ... ' her admirers echoed.

'Cocksuckers,' Eleanor retorted, trying out one of the many stateside curses imported by her cousin Tom.

Louise laughed and winked over the heads of her admirers.

One day in the goosepimpling cold of the cloakroom, Louise approached Eleanor where she sat alone, gnawing a biscuit.

'Can I have a bite?'

Eleanor held out the biscuit.

'Thanks.' Louise paced between the rows of drooping coats. 'I was looking for you,' she said, heeling around at the end of one aisle. 'Why do you eat lunch in here?'

'Because I like it.'

'It's disgusting,' Louise snorted.

Under the beautiful girl's attention Eleanor felt her body shrivel like plastic in a fire.

'It pongs of smelly socks.'

'I don't mind.'

Louise stepped up and slid one foot before the other along the bench until she reached Eleanor and crouched beside her.

'What does it feel like?'

'What?'

'Your funny arm.'

'Cold, most of the time.' Eleanor shrugged, masking her gratitude for this attention. 'And as if someone is dragging it, trying to pull me backwards.'

Louise draped her arm behind her back in imitation of Eleanor's natural pose. When she remembered to, Eleanor would lift her arm forward and fold it into the crook of the other, or cradle the elbow like an egg in her palm.

'I see what you mean, ' Louise said. 'It feels weird. Do you hate it?'

Eleanor shrugged again. 'Sometimes. When people pity me.'

Martialled by the handbell, the two girls sauntered back to class. Louise hooked Eleanor's numb arm. Warmth spiralled through the smaller girl.

'Maureen says you killed her rabbit.'

'I didn't. I set him free but the neighbour's cat got him.'

'Maureen is thick. She looks thick, too, with all those hairy moles.'

'Slugs.'

Louise sniggered. 'What did she need a rabbit for when she had all those chappies on her face?'

'Moley-poley,' Eleanor laughed.

An hour later a jotter page folded small as a dice landed on the battle of Clontarf. Sneaking it into her lap, Eleanor read:

Can you come to my house for tea on Saturday?
No funny bunnies. No moley-poleys.

Love
Louise

With a flourish, she had intertwined the LS of love and Louise. Eleanor refolded her first love letter and hid it in her pencil case.

Rust searing the curve of a stone dolphin's grin burnt down to a dry blue basin bespattered with leaves and paper. But for the wooden plaque marked 'Hellas' with a funny A, Eleanor might have turned away, imagining the house to be empty. Her knock was answered by a small boy, his mouth painted to a perfect carmine bow. Wordless, he bolted up the stairs, and a moment later Louise appeared on the landing, a towel turbanning her head.

'Mary's polishing my nails,' she explained as Eleanor mounted towards her. 'She'll do yours next if you like.'

In the fug of damp hair and cheap cosmetics Tom Jones was hankering for the green, green grass of home. The housekeeper, her hair also wrapped in a towel, sat cross-legged in a pink nylon dressing gown on the bed. Squinting back a curl of cigarette smoke, she nodded and motioned Eleanor into a chair entrailed with underwear. The child gripped the edge of the seat, avoiding the suspender grips and a panty girdle.

'No, Stavvy,' Mary shrieked. 'For the last time – I'm not doing your nails. Your mammy'd have me guts for garters.' She crushed her cigarette in a saucer and returned to her task.

Louise suddenly twitched, and reaching under the bed, pulled out a pile of dog-eared magazines which she piled into Eleanor's lap.

'Now pretend you're waiting in the hairdresser's.'

'Stavvy, I'm warning you.' Mary lunged across the bed, but the boy squirmed away, clasping the varnish bottle.

'I'll get him.' Louise sprang to bar the door and dropped her brother with a kick in the shin.

Like a rejected heart, the wedge-shaped bottle bounced onto the floor. The boy doubled, sobbing into his knees.

Eleanor concentrated on the magazines while Mary's voice chorused with Sandy Shaw until it collapsed into a fit of coughing.

'The legs of a sparrow and she couldn't sing a note,' she gasped.

'When I'm an actress, I'll sing and dance,' Louise declared.

'More power to ye, girl.'

Other voices were besieging Eleanor from the tea-ringed pages of the magazines, where women fretted about vaginal itch and heavy petting and boyfriends who wouldn't propose. She squirmed at her own fascination with these intimacies. The magazines slid to the floor but the worries clung to her like an odour.

'Look' – Louise fanned her vermilion nails – 'now

you can get yours done, modom.'

'No thanks.'

'Go on,' Louise pressed. 'I'm going to do my toe-nails too.'

Mary lit a fresh cigarette. 'Is yer pal having no beauty treatment today?'

'No. Don't mind her. She's only a smelly Nelly.'

'All right,' Eleanor relented, 'you can do my toe-nails.'

'Only if yer feet's clean,' Mary warned.

Petula Clark headed downtown.

The weight of the polish on her toes surprised Eleanor and when she looked at them her feet seemed to grow away from her.

'Moses supposes his toeses are roses but Moses supposes erroneously,' Mary chanted.

'You might as well get your fingernails done now,' Louise said, 'because they don't match your toes any more.'

Eleanor's fingers were transmogrified by the polished nails.

'What happened to this one, love?' Mary dandled the distorted hand.

'Nothing.'

'She was in a car crash and her parents were killed,' Louise recited simply.

'That's very sad.'

Eleanor dropped her eyes to escape Mary's pity.

'Coronation Red,' Mary said for distraction.

Louise plucked the bottle from her hand. '*Carnation*, not *coronation*,' she mocked. 'It's a flower.'

'I know that. Like what a groom wears in his

buttonhole.' Mary closed her eyes, and hugging her ribs, swayed in sync with Cliff Richard.

On an impulse Louise started up and flung the bottle at her brother, who was still huddled in the corner by the door. He ducked and the bottle hit the wall.

Eleanor flinched at the sound of breaking glass.

'Ye bloody little в,' Mary bawled.

Convulsed with giggles, Stavvy darted out of the room.

'Get out, the whole lot of yous.' Mary stumped to the corner and began gingerly gathering the fragments. 'Here.' She paused and swivelled on her hunkers. 'I've an idea. Bring us the remover.'

Louise fumbled among the smeary bottles on the dressing table, and finding the right one, handed it to Mary, who blotted the stain.

'Mother of God, it's taking the pattern off too.'

'But that's not so bad.'

'Well at least yer mammy won't think I was doing holy murder in here.'

'I was going to tell her it was Nelly's fault,' Louise taunted.

'Then you're a liar.' Eleanor's new fingers bunched into a fist.

'Out now, and let me get dressed in peace.'

'We can help you, Mary.' Louise embraced her waist and tickled her.

Mary gurgled. 'I don't need your help.'

'Race you to the garden, Nelly,' Louise cried, fleeing the room.

'And get some shoes on you,' Mary called after her,

but the tail of Louise's hair, loosed from its turban, whipped around the newel post and disappeared.

Outside, Eleanor found her hostess circling the lawn on a navy and white bicycle. At the foot of the garden Stavvy had fallen into rhythmic digging with a trowel.

'Here, Nelly,' Louise shouted, 'you have a go.'

Eleanor refused.

'Come on, it's easy.' Louise spun to a blur on the lawn's sunny area.

Just when Eleanor thought her friend must fly, the bike wavered to a stop. 'Why won't you try, Nelly?'

'My name's not Nelly.'

'Oh *Eleanor*, then.'

Eleanor gnawed her lip and eventually raised her crooked arm.

'That's nothing,' Louise said. 'I can ride with no hands. Come on, I'll help you.'

Her guest drew back.

'Come on.' Louise led her onto the lawn.

Fleet at Eleanor's side, Louise steered the bike in circles, then released it. Catching the momentum, Eleanor ignored her crippled arm, and pedalling hard, abandoned herself to the giddy surge of speed. Her friend's calls dwindled to a babble as the garden spun its greens and her head whistled into space. When she fell the sky continued to spin like a juggler's dish. She choked, waiting for her breath to return and for Louise to haul the bike off her legs.

'Oh bloody Mary.' Louise's hands flew to her mouth.

A red ooze trailed over Eleanor's ankle. Leaning forward, she saw a flap of skin raised off the joint. The blood seeped smoothly into her white sock and reached her shoe.

'I'll get you a plaster.' Louise ran into the house and returned with a length of gauze which she wrapped around the wound. 'Now you'll have to go and play heroes with Stavvy.'

Obediently, Eleanor hobbled to the end of the garden while Louise remounted the bike. Stavvy was bent over a deep burrow. To one side of him was a cascading mound of clay, on the other, a scattering of porcelain shards, a blackened coin, a doll's shoe and a bent spoon.

'What are you looking for?' Eleanor crouched beside him.

'Nothing,' Stavvy grunted.

'I fell off the bike.'

'Huh.'

'Louise said I was to play heroes with you.'

'You don't have to do everything she says.'

'Well, what'll I do?'

'Couldn't care less.' He raised the trowel, balancing a worm on its edge. When the worm fell he clove it in two, a grin sliding over his lips as the halves curled and parted. 'Spaghetti.'

Eleanor stood up and wandered towards the dump. Decay sweltered off the pile of yellowing grass. The voice of a boy entreating his dog splashed up from the neighbouring garden. Tippy-toed on the heap, Eleanor peeped over the wall to see a mutt lathered with soapsuds streaking through flowerbeds and the boy in laughing pursuit. She frowned and stepped down.

'Where are you going?' Louise called as Eleanor marched up the garden.

'Home.'

Indoors, Mary tried to make Eleanor change her mind. 'I'll call Louise and the two of ye can have a glass of orange and some biscuits.'

Eleanor was adamant.

'All right, so.' Mary led her into the hall. 'Do you know the number?'

'Yes.' She waited until the phone rang out, imagining its shrill piercing the empty house.

Louise joined her as she replaced the receiver. 'Are you going home?'

'No.'

'Good. You're never to do that again.' She ran her fingers through Eleanor's short hair. 'You can be my best friend.'

Eleanor's nodding acquiescence hid the pride which suffused her.

Swinging into Louise's sashay, she followed the call of Nashville to the kitchen.

Eye to the keyhole of the locked garden gate, Eleanor watched the river flush its groove with the leap of spring while behind the windows of the bakery on the opposite bank the risen loaves trundled their tireless circle. Angela, straightening against her hoe, called Eleanor, and when the child stood beside her, stooped to meet her eyes.

'Are you happy in our family?' she asked.

Eleanor pondered the question.

'You know we love you.'

'I suppose so,' she mumbled.

'Well, we do. Now I want to show you something.' From her cardigan pocket Angela drew a corm no bigger than a wisdom tooth. 'You know the way flowers grow?' She began.

'Yes.'

'Well babies grow the same way. Inside their mummies.'

Eleanor's nose wrinkled. 'Are you going to eat that?'

'No.' Angela smiled. 'The daddy puts the seed into the mummy.'

'You mean when they fuck?'

The woman's expression revulsed. 'Where did you pick that up?'

'At school.'

'It's a filthy word. Never use it again.'

Eleanor stared at the pronged corm. 'Are you going to have a baby?'

'Yes.'

'When?'

'In August.'

That night Eleanor clambered onto a chair and hauled her suitcase off the top of the wardrobe. With her finger she traced the label gummed to its lid. ISLE OF MAN. The words revolved on three crooked legs. Snapping it open, she contemplated its watermarked lining and ran her finger round the puckered inner pocket still gritty with holiday sand. She packed her parents' photo album, the strand of her father's hair, his old song book and her musty rosary beads and put the suitcase back on top of the wardrobe.

From the outset Aoife's rolling gaze deflected Eleanor's stare.

'Smile at her,' Angela advised.

Eleanor smirked but the baby's lids closed.

Ronan fell in love with his new sister. 'She's laughing,' he enthused when a ripple of wind flexed the inchoate face. He wiggled her fingers and toes and jounced her on his knee till she spewed.

'I beg your puddin'!' Dermot exclaimed and called Angela to clean their daughter.

Angela invited Eleanor to help bathe the infant but the girl was repelled by the short slithery limbs.

'You'll have to learn sometime,' Angela said.

'No I won't.' Eleanor shook off that certainty.

'Don't be like that, lovey,' Angela sighed.

Eleanor walked away, pulling a face at the baby, whose head wobbled over Angela's shoulder.

Mrs Tighe chucked the baby under the chin. 'Isn't she the spit of Dermot?' She widened her overpainted lips to win confirmation from her husband.

'She's got his nose, all right.' Syl Tighe nodded in his granddaughter's direction. 'But I hope she has better legs. That's what'll count in the long run, isn't that so?' He winked at Ronan, adding, 'You'll be bringing home the babies any day now.'

Ronan flushed.

'Syl, stop it,' his wife scolded.

'Don't be making me old before my time,' Dermot protested.

'Yes, the living spit.' Mrs Tighe's tone tightened the maternal cordon around her daughter and grand-daughter, estranging the men. Eleanor hovered in the gap between them.

'There it is,' Louise cried, pointing at punch-drunk balloons tied to a gatepost.

Angela kerbed the car. 'Have a nice time.'

'We will.'

Eleanor bounced across the back seat after her friend, but Louise had skipped to the top of the stone steps and was already tapping the brass lion paw.

'Ooh. Your dress is beautiful,' crowed Julie in greeting.

Louise twirled across the hall till her pleats flared and the silk embroidery on her bolero minnowed in the sunlight spilling through the open door. White pompons bobbled from her sock tops.

'Mum and Dad brought it from Athens.'

'You lucky thing.'

Eleanor saw suddenly how easy it would be to hate Louise. 'Happy birthday, Julie,' she said, her shadow slanting over the threshold.

'Thank you, Eleanor.' Adding the latest gifts to the stack of parcels, Julie led her guests out to the garden.

Jostling in a crush of frocks, the party girls smiled at Louise's arrival and opened a space for her.

'Look, Mummy,' Julie called. 'Isn't Louise's dress beautiful?'

'Yes, darling,' Mrs Barry said. 'Now, why don't you line up for the races?'

'You're all as pretty as flowers,' sang out Julie's Aunt Trish.

Soon, with their skirts tucked into their knickers like galligaskins, the children were sprinting the length of the lawn, essaying bamboo-staked long and high jumps. Thwarted by these, Eleanor was charged with helping Aunt Trish adjust the poles, and at five o'clock, while her companions crowded indoors for tea, she was detained to dismantle the jumps.

'You're a great girl.' Aunt Trish beamed prodigally when they were finished.

In the dining room hands swarmed over sandwiches and crisps, stabbed cocktail sticks into chubby sausages, pulled the wings off butterfly cakes and laid waste a glistening fleet of jelly boats. Afterwards, a cake aureoled with light swam into the glutted darkness.

The birthday chant sighed away when Julie failed to blow out all twelve candles.

'Now you won't get your wish,' Maureen gloated.

Aunt Trish embraced her niece. 'She has all she wants and more – isn't that so?'

Julie nodded, but when the curtains opened again the shimmer of Louise's bolero teased her eye.

Clapping her hands for silence, Mrs Barry announced a beetle drive.

'Have you done a beetle drive before?' Aunt Trish

bent towards Eleanor.

She shook her head.

Louise rolled her eyes to the ceiling and said, 'Well, you haven't missed anything. It's bloody boring.'

'Louise Makarios.' Aunt Trish quivered. 'What would your mother say?'

'She'd probably agree.'

Eleanor giggled.

'Why can't we have a disco?' Louise began to grind her hips, chanting, ' "I can't get no satisfaction".'

'That's not very nice,' Aunt Trish reproved.

'You're only an old prude, Trish.'

Taken aback, the woman stiffened her shoulders and left the room.

'Her and her bloody beetles.' Louise sniggered. 'Let her go and stick legs on them. Actually, Mum says it's training for bridge nights.'

'Ugh.' Eleanor grimaced. 'Angela has those. Dermot calls it the witches' coven.'

'What's a coven?'

'When witches sit around and make spells.'

'That sounds like fun.'

'But they only ever play cards and eat cakes.'

Louise's face curled to a scheming grin, and whispering to her friend, she suggested that they hide until the game had started, then come down and scoff the rest of the party tea.

As they snuck downstairs from their refuge they were stalled by the sight of Trish in the hall. Wedged at the open door, she was saying 'no, no, no', her yellow perm jiggling with the emphatic twist of her head.

'Even a crust, ma'am,' a small voice wheedled.

'Oh, very well.' Trish sighed. 'Wait there.' She shut the door, and eyes darting from side to side, scurried into the dining room.

Louise and Eleanor sat back and watched through the banister rails. Moments later Aunt Trish reappeared carrying a paper plate arrayed with sandwiches and cakes.

'Now, dear,' she whispered, passing the platter out. 'But don't call here again. Do you understand?'

'Trish!' Mrs Barry's voice froze her at the door.

'Yes, Noreen.'

'I thought I told you not to encourage those brats.'

Trish spun round to meet her sister's reproach. 'What harm is it? There's so much left over' – one hand flailed in the direction of the dining room – 'besides, I told her not to come back.'

'Sometimes I despair of you. How can you be so naïve?'

Trish smarted.

'We'll have the whole wretched family in on top of us.'

'I'm sorry, Noreen. I know you're right. I must be more cautious.' Distractedly, she wiped a straggle of hair from her forehead. 'It was just ... the party and everything ... I was a little flustered.'

'All right,' Mrs Barry relented. 'Come on and join the girls. Can you believe they're almost young women?'

As soon as the coast was clear, Eleanor and Louise tiptoed into the dining room.

From the window they saw the tinker crouch beneath a laburnum tree inside the gate.

'She's doing number two,' Louise hooted.

Eleanor craned over her friend's shoulder. 'Mrs Barry will have a fit.'

'Here, let's wave at her.' Louise flung up the sash and leaned out.

Seeing them, the girl stood, arms akimbo, and called up. 'What are yous staring at?'

'Do you want another cake?'

The girl declined but Louise was already poised with a cherry cake, which flew over the drive to land at the trespasser's feet. Having considered the manna for a moment, the girl picked it up, bit halfway through, flung the other half away and wandered off. Set under the tree, Trish's alms now steamed with the addition of two straw-coloured turds.

'Trish is for it,' Eleanor said.

'That's what she gets for being an old maid.'

'Well, Mrs Barry is a B.'

'Yeah. Anyway, I'm not going to be an old maid.'

'Are you going to get married? And have children?'

'You bet.'

'I don't think I will.'

'Oh yes you will.' Louise crammed a chocolate éclair into her mouth. 'Unless you're up the pole and have the babies before.'

'What do you mean?'

'That's what Mary calls it. You know –' Louise joined the finger and thumb of her left hand and wiggled her right index finger through the circle. 'When you do it before you get married.'

'I don't believe you.' Eleanor blushed, shy of an unfamiliar itch teasing between her legs.

When her first blood showed, Eleanor watched the water in the toilet bowl redden like seepage from a slaughterhouse. Her whole abdomen appeared to be dripping away, as throughout the week thick clots lowered themselves on fine red threads from her vagina. Her thighs felt as if they were clamped with steel and she waddled like an invalid with the ST strapped between her legs, casting her eye over her shoulder every now and then for fear that stains might betray her condition.

Schoolmates called it 'the curse' but Angela explained the process as the womb's preparation for a baby.

'I don't want a baby,' Eleanor complained.

'One day you will.'

'Do you have to get married to have a baby?'

'Yes.'

'What if you're up the pole?'

'Eleanor!' Exasperation wearied Angela's voice. 'Sometimes people who are not married do have babies. But that's a sin.'

When Eleanor shared Angela's womb theory with Louise, her friend laughed. Quickly on her fingers she made a calculation. 'That means in your life you get ready for nearly four hundred babies!'

Eleanor paled.

'Of course, to have one takes nine months, so in fact you could only have about thirty-five,' Louise reassured her. 'Unless they were twins or triplets, then you might have seventy or one hundred and fifteen.'

Anger burnt in Eleanor. 'I hate babies.'

Some weeks later, on her return from school, Eleanor found an assortment of bras displayed on her bed.

'I took them out on appro.' Angela fondled the scalloped cups on one sample. 'Won't you try them on?'

Eleanor flung her satchel onto her desk and began to pull out exercise books.

'You have to wear one, dear ...' Angela's hands reached to weigh the young breasts.

Eleanor shrank away.

'... Otherwise you'll sag and look like an old woman by the time you're twenty. Besides, you'll be more comfortable.'

'All right.'

'Good.' Angela sat on the bed.

Eleanor rolled her eyes. 'Later.'

As a birthday treat that year, Angela planned to re-decorate Eleanor's bedroom. She moved in with Aoife while the painter's impersonation of Rod

Stewart echoed in the stripped room. Aoife's wide-set stare followed Eleanor as she wedged her large suitcase under the camp bed.

'Will you read me a story tonight?'

'OK. Just one.'

Aoife swung off her bed to kneel beside the bookshelves, gravely removing and opening each volume until she found *The Stolen Child* and handed it to Eleanor.

Each afternoon, as soon as he came home, Ronan rushed to find his little sister, swung her onto his shoulder and produced a lollipop or liquorice pipe for her to suck. He met Eleanor's greeting with a grunt and bore Aoife to his room, where her giddy peals rose over his laugh. Eleanor stretched on the camp bed, ears wrapped in the pillow, seeking the oblivion of sleep.

Yet night by night, embayed in the glow from a bedside lamp, Aoife and Eleanor became friends. Rereading the old storybooks, Eleanor traced the distance she had travelled from childhood. Seeing its happier counterpart in this child, she regretted her own lost self and dreaded the transition to come. When Aoife slept against her shoulder, Eleanor dipped her lips to the placid brow.

At the top of the stairs the birthday parade halted to make way for the new thirteen-year-old. Eleanor was pressed forward to open the bedroom door. Cornflower-sprigged light billowed before her, a breeze lifting the muslin blind which, in place of the window bars, blurred the garden. Thirteen long-stemmed red buds strained from a vase on the dressing table, their blood darkness an affront to the myriad sweet blooms covering the walls and bed. Eleanor's eye slid to the figure cramped in the mirror. Who is the girl they want to live here? she asked the reflection.

'Are you pleased? Do you like it?' Angela simmered over the threshold.

'Yeah.'

'Look in the wardrobe.' Angela's embrace urged her towards the cupboard. 'Isn't it a pretty colour?'

Face tricked to show pleasure, Eleanor's fingers played over the cotton smock and noted the matching shawl, so certainly intended to protect the world from her disfigurement.

'I wish I was you.' Aoife bounced on the bed.

'Don't dirty the new quilt,' Angela scolded. Returning to her husband's side, she nestled against his arm. 'The roses are from Dermot.'

'That's right. For a blue lady.'

'She's not blue. She's happy.'

Under the odour of forced flowers the whiff of asepsis dehumanised the room where Eleanor's grandmother lay, her woolly hair scraped back to disappear into the starch-white pillow. Her breath rasped. Beside the bed her two remaining brothers counted off Gran's last moments in the Hail Marys of the Sorrowful Mysteries. Impatient with the monotonous recital, Eleanor pushed through to the bedside and played her fingers over the dying woman's face. One of the old men touched her shoulder to draw her away. She shrugged him off and bent closer to the pillow, willing her grandmother's eyes to open.

'Gran, Gran,' she whispered, 'I brought you daffodils.'

The rasping hastened into a momentary calm and the milky eyes cleared. Eleanor smiled, encouraging the recognition that flared, then passed. She brushed her face to the wilted cheek, where warmth continued to pulse, not knowing that life had slipped away.

★

Moonlight blued the room where Eleanor and her grandmother had sat, week in, week out, for as long as she could remember. Absence already chilled the air. Eleanor filled the mould of the old woman's shape in the chair facing the garden. She held the memory box on her knee, conscious for the first time of how light it was. But how do you weigh a life? she thought as she unwrapped the cherished objects.

Closing her eyes, she reached for those lost lives: she riffled the pages of the missal, held the broken eggshell to her ear, drew her father's baby hair across her lips, but she remained numb. Their resonance had faded. Opening her eyes, she saw the garden reversed by night.

'I tried at first to live by the memory of what I had seen,' Gran was saying again. 'Then I realised that I was only making a prison for myself. Expecting nothing to change. I had to relearn the world. Find my way through it again.'

Eleanor lifted the box off her knee. She lit a small fire in the grate and one by one she cast the husks of memory into the flames, withholding only the bullet, which she tucked into the pocket of her jeans. When the flames had sifted to embers she sneaked out, as she had come in, by the french window. The absolute blank of the world before dawn shook her heart.

Recalled from Africa, Ray became a frequent visitor at the O'Driscolls' home. Eleanor clung to him as a personal possession, able in his presence to ignore Ronan's taciturnity, but knifed by jealousy when he played with Aoife. Impetuously, she would beg her uncle to take her for a spin on his bike. Dermot would seize Angela's wrist to stay her objections.

Her spastic hand secured in the pocket of the priest's black anorak, the other clamped to his waist, Eleanor brightened with the folly of speed. Not that the second-hand Yamaha 200 was a streak, but braced on its engine, dipping as it cornered, winged by the open breeze, she was happy. She usually chose to stop first at the graveyard. Ray helped her to clear weeds from her parents' bed, then strolled off towards the derelict chapel or across the road to the seafront, leaving her seated on the headstone to talk to Colm and Margaret. She asked the old questions: why had they abandoned her? what was her crime? where had they gone? Spun out, she sat, indifferent to the tears streaking her face, and waited for the placatory silence of the grave, more actual than voices, to replenish her.

Afterwards Eleanor and Ray walked for a while, then swung back into Raheny for a feed of burgers and chips. Plucking one of the vinegared wedges from the greaseproof bag, Ray passed it under his nose like the finest hand-rolled Havana.

'The one thing I never stopped missing out there' — he wagged the half-bitten chip at Eleanor — 'I used to wake in the middle of the night, panting for a good soggy bag of them.'

'I'm thinking of giving up meat.' She eyed the congealing remains of her burger.

'Why?'

'The look of it, the smell of it. The blood, I think. It's like eating used tampons.'

'Stop. I was just going to polish off your burger.'

'Is the food horrible in your place?'

'Not really. I feel hungry all the time here. Maybe it's the cold or the boredom of being in limbo.'

She hunched forward. 'Do you think those places exist — limbo, purgatory, heaven, hell?'

'I do.' He tossed a match into the foil ashtray.

Eleanor forked her fingers for a pull on his cigarette. 'I can't imagine them. But I feel like my body is the wrong fit' — her hand clawed the air — 'and the right one is out there. Sometimes it comes close, like *déjà vu*. You know, coming back on yourself.'

'I accept life as a gift and I cherish it because of the giver. The imperfections come from being careless of it.'

'Is God like a person for you?'

'No.' Ray considered. 'I see Him as a great fountain of light, where all pain and confusion ends.'

'Then you want to die.'

'No. But I have to earn my death.'

'Do you ever stop believing?'

'Occasionally. And I sink – like Saint Peter.' Pushing back his chair, Ray stood. 'Time to go.'

'You hate being home, don't you?'

'It's not home any more, Eleanor,' he said. 'Nowhere is home – or everywhere is home. God is home.'

'That's sad.'

'No, it's not.' He pulled on his anorak. 'Come on, or Angela will think we're lost.'

'He's gorgeous.'

    'Who?'

'Your uncle, stupo.' Louise craned to watch the bike swing onto the road.

    'He's a priest.'

    'So?'

    'So you can't make eyes at him.'

    'Ha!' Louise scoffed. 'You should hear what Mary says about the priest in her town.'

    'Well, he's different.'

    'Mary,' Louise called up the stairs.

    The voice of John Denver yodelled back.

    Louise cupped her hands around her mouth. 'M-a-r-y.'

    'What is it?' Mary blundered onto the landing.

    'Did you see Nelly's uncle?'

    Mary's eyes popped as she shook her head.

    'He's a hunk. He brought her over on his motor-bike.'

    'Why didn't ye invite him in?'

Eleanor sighed. 'He's a priest.'

'Oh.' Mary's face sagged. 'It's as well ye didn't then – he might have been tempted,' she preened and returned to her room.

'She wants me to go to the party as Tammy Wynette.' Louise pulled a face. 'D-I-V-O-R-C-E.' Hips clicking on each letter, she led her friend to the kitchen. 'I'd prefer to be Eva Peron or Bianca Jagger.'

'I don't know what to go as.'

'You could be "The Fugitive".'

'Bitch.'

'What about Helen Keller? Except you'd be bumping into people all night.'

'Nana Mouskouri would suit you.'

'Funny ha-ha.' Louise stirred two mugs of coffee. 'Mother's on another fecking diet so we've no biscuits.'

'What about Joni Mitchell?'

'Janis Joplin?'

'Dana?'

'. . . sailboats and dishymen . . .' Louise lisped.

Eleanor said, 'I give up.'

'Although Janis Joplin's not bad. I could wear three of Mum's hats and her fur coat.'

'She'd never let you.'

Finger pressed to her lips, Louise wagged her head. 'Anyway she's too busy running around with her little boyfriends to notice.'

'OK. But what about me?'

'The orange hair is a problem.' Louise paused. 'Lucille Ball or Queen Elizabeth I.'

'Shut up.'

'I know –' Louise flashed. '– Bowie. Mary could paint your face.'

'Yeah.' Eleanor grinned as Aladdin Sane's lightning bolt split her face. 'Yeah, that's good.'

'I always knew you were depraved.'

Louise maintained that the bad weather was what made the Irish inward looking. She moaned about the damp and the dark, and vowed to return to Greece, where her father owned a piece of land on the side of a mountain.

'You can come with me, Nelly, and dance naked in the sun.'

'But you're Irish too,' Eleanor pointed out.

'Only half. Anyway nationality comes from the father.'

'Says who?'

'Moi.'

'My father said Ireland was only half a nation.'

'Oh blessèd Saint Colm. Look where it got him.'

'He died in an *accident*.'

'And *your* accident was to survive.'

'What's that supposed to mean?'

'You carry death around like a bad smell.'

Eleanor sniffed her underarm. 'No, only sweat and Mum.'

'You're yella, Nelly. Your folks are gone and they'll never be got. You're on your own. Jesus, sometimes I wish I was.'

Eleanor's protest faltered. There was a truth in Louise's words that she feared. She was drowning outside herself.

'I'll find a nice young Yanni to put a stop to your moaning.' Louise licked her lips.

Eleanor was to see Greece sooner than she imagined. The Makarioses were renting a villa in Naxos for the month of August and Louise invited her friend to join them for a fortnight.

Angela frowned. 'I'll have to discuss it with Dermot.'

Craned over the banisters that night, Eleanor heard her foster parents' exchange.

'Why not?' Dermot was protesting. 'You're being petty.'

'Well, there's the expense.'

'The air fare and pocket money – we can manage that.'

'She'll need new clothes.'

'A bikini.'

'You have a blind spot where that girl is concerned.'

'Go to bed, Angela. We'll talk when you can think straight.'

'Don't speak that way to me.'

Newspaper crackled.

'And don't hide.'

'Look, Angela. I've no idea what's eating you but

you've no right to take it out on Eleanor. I'll pay for her holiday and I'll buy her clothes. So you forget about it.'

'And what about *our* children? Have you forgotten them?'

'Are you jealous, Angela?' His incredulity heightened. 'You do all right. I give you nice things, we go to Spain every year – we can take the kids this year if you like.'

'I'm sick of Spain.'

'What is it you want of me, Angela?'

'I don't know, Dermot. I don't know.'

Eleanor withdrew. She knew that Angela was right. Dermot did favour her but without slight to his own children. He opened to her, as strangers travelling together will swap unexpected intimacies.

'I was going to rid the world of skulduggery.' He laughed. 'The intrepid stringer. Then I met Angela and settled for a "steady job". In fact, she found it for me.'

'I would hate someone who wanted me to change,' Eleanor said.

'Society runs on compromise.' His arm swung to encompass the other Sunday strollers in the park.

'I don't see the difference between that and hypocrisy.'

'You're too narrow in your judgements. You'll wind up miserable.'

'Are you happy?'

'Don't ask me that.' He drew a long breath. 'I'm content.'

'Keep your head down and avoid all questions.' She scuffed a pebble down the path.

'Sometimes I think you were sent to try us.'

'Maybe I was.'

'You didn't lick that off the ground.' Dermot laughed and continued cautiously. 'Don't misunderstand me, now, but maybe Colm was fated in a way. He was so fierce. Compromise would have suffocated him.'

Eleanor heeled around to meet Dermot's eye. 'You have no right to say that.'

Dermot bowed and nodded glumly. 'Yes, you're right. Forgive me?' His eyes cast sidelong to hers. 'I suppose we're always trying to explain death away. Or our own part in it.'

'Don't waste your breath,' she said, and plunged into the shade of a pergola.

A week after the row with Angela, Dermot asked Eleanor to work on the paper to earn the price of her trip to Greece. She was to start as a runner, on Saturdays, until school was out and then do three days a week through June and July. She loved those days. Stepping into the print room was like entering the hold of a ship. She tried to mask her confusion at the ricochet of wolf whistles. In the features room she was tickled by the siren announcing the arrival of copy and she laughed as she delivered the tight little scrolls to the appropriate desks. A sports writer crowned her with a baseball cap. Soon the pass-remarkable stares and nudges subsided and the girl with the crooked arm and the white hat was accorded the indifference of familiarity.

Between chores she prodded one-fingered at the keys of a heavy black typewriter. Late one afternoon a pair of arms curved around her shoulders and a set of hairy ink-stained fingers dabbled the keys to produce the sentence: 'The quick brown fox jumped over the lazy dog.'

She laughed. Swiftly another sentence appeared: 'Eleanor Leyden is amused.'

She tipped back against the man's paunch to see his face.

'I'll give you lessons the next day you're in.' He smiled, and, hitching a red and white Manchester United bag onto his shoulder, lumbered away.

In the car that evening she told Dermot of the offer.

'Good. Who was it?'

'I don't know.'

'Are you getting a taste for the newspaper business?'

'It's more fun than school.'

'Ronan's too precious for it,' Dermot said. 'Doesn't like to get his hands dirty.'

'Well, it is pretty grubby in there.'

'In more ways than one,' he conceded. 'But we'll be modernising one day: word processors and computers – if the unions let us. Although I'll be almost sorry. I like the ink on my paws, muck under the fingernails: evidence of a day's labour.'

Eleanor lived now from Saturday to Saturday.

ELEANOR LEYDEN FOR PRESIDENT

LEYDEN FLIES TO CAMP DAVID

NO SURRENDER, SAYS LEYDEN

Every week the headlines stood against the platen of the typewriter commandeered for her lesson. Frank, her tutor, ignored his mates' teasing as she bent to the keys.

'It looks like the house style,' jibed one man at her gobbledegook.

There were days when she caught the tail end of a resentful susurrus as soon as her white cap bobbed between the desks.

'Don't mind them,' Frank muttered one afternoon. 'They wouldn't trust their own mothers.'

She recognised in their mood the schoolroom cold shoulder for telltales, but was at a loss to understand their fear until a question of Dermot's, dropped into their conversation, gave her an inkling.

'I wonder whether you hear talk of industrial action

on your rounds.'

'No.'

'I'm not asking you to spy. But there are some agi-
tators who are against change. If they're not careful,
there'll be no jobs at all. It's dog eat dog out there.'

Eleanor stared out of the car to find this world of
raging beasts but the passers-by were bent on catching
the next bus. The aggressive tic working in Dermot's
face diminished him. She wondered at how life had
fetched her up alongside this stranger on this of all
thronged streets.

ELEANOR LEYDEN HAS MASSIVE EYES

Bowing to hide her flush, Eleanor tore the sentence from the page and pushed it into her pocket. In mid-leap the quick brown fox was halted by her teacher's hands.

'I didn't mean to embarrass you,' he was saying as he composed a fresh sentence on the keys.

She heated under the pressure of his weight on her shoulders. Without reading the words printed there, her eyes steadied on the paper. Only when Frank had returned to his desk did she understand that he was inviting her out.

'Would you like to come to the International on Saturday?'

'Yes,' her finger tapped.

It was the last match of the season. The national anthem was baffled by the wind but her voice rose to chant the phrases whose sense she had lost. Frank, miming a grimace, stopped his ears. As soon as the ball went into play a sea change converted the crowd to a unanimous roar. From the press seats near the pitch Eleanor could hear the thud of tackling bodies and see the iron rake of the players' faces daubed with mud. The roar swung from one side of the pitch to the other. In the stands behind Eleanor and Frank a Cork man's jeers punctuated the afternoon.

'Go home, you joke!' he cried, and swayed on tipsy feet to abuse the Dublin hooker.

'Are you enjoying it?' Frank nudged Eleanor during half-time.

She smiled, tucking her chin into the folds of her scarf.

'Here, I brought a flask.' He rummaged in his canvas holdall and served her a milky coffee and a Club Milk.

'That's like Mary Poppins's bag.' She laughed through the warm cloud rising off her cup.

Frank laughed with her and smoothed her hair. 'Sure you're not too cold?'

She nodded, and as the crowd surged again, fixed her eyes on the returning players to steady the blur which Frank excited in her. When he moved close, desire astonished her groin. She didn't give a toss about the game. Instead she saw herself and Frank naked, stuck into one another on the muddy pitch, and laughed. He turned to her, eyebrows raised. She shook her head.

Louise would have sniggered at Frank. He was nothing like the fellas she toyed with outside the shop after school and in Bewley's on Saturday mornings. The boy she was throwing her cap at had a hawkish face framed by limp curling hair, and a smile under-scored by a leer. Frank had years on that skinny-malinks.

'Probably a dirty old man,' Louise had snorted when Eleanor mentioned the typing lessons.

'Does he wear a raincoat?' Full of wisdom regarding the raincoat brigade, she relayed Mary's caution-ary tale about the man in the mac who had driven her home from a dance. He tried to get off with Mary, but just before they kissed she spotted a baby's bottle on the back seat. Outraged, she sprang from the car, tore off her shoe and smashed the windscreen with the heel. The next day Louise saw the crumbs of glass on the road.

Eleanor hadn't mentioned Frank again to her friend but she was relieved when he had turned up in a sheepskin coat.

Frank grinned when she refused a beer and chose a Coke.

Peeved, she said, 'What's so funny?'

'Nothing.' He shook his head. 'Except I think that's what I like about you, Red.'

'What?'

'The way you don't much care what anyone thinks.'

'Don't I?'

'You seem not to.'

She stared into her black drink. She felt as though he had unzipped her and made her look at her own entrails. She squirmed.

His pint glass tapped her tumbler. 'Wakey-wakey.'

She drank long, concentrating on him. He remained unknown to her.

'So, have you had enough rugby to do you a life-time?'

'I wouldn't go that far. Do you play?'

'No. I went to an Irish school. Sasanach games were out. What about − ?'

'They don't know what to do with me at PE class, unless we're pretending to be flowers or doing the polka.'

'I'd like to see you being a flower,' he laughed.

'I make a nice rose,' she said.

He smiled and licked beer froth off his lips.

Escorting her out, he diligently shielded her weak side from the jostle. He walked her to the end of Anglesea Road.

'You don't have to see me to the door,' she said.

'All right,' he said, understanding what was with-held from parents. 'See you next week.'

'Yep.' She waited.

'Bye, so.'

'Bye.'

He turned toward the city centre.

'Hey, Frank.' Her call halted him. 'Thanks.'

He bowed from across the bridge. 'My pleasure, Eleanor Leyden.'

E leanor was startled when Frank's tongue first rummaged in her mouth. Its progress round her teeth stalled as she quivered.

'Are you all right?'

'Yes.' The huskiness of her voice surprised her. She swallowed back the sour aftertaste of his beer. 'I had the hiccups,' she apologised as her hand encouraged his broad face to approach hers again.

None of Louise's expertise had prepared her for the maddening of her belly and thighs. Frank's mouth widened and this time his tongue filled her mouth. The ache died away and her tongue began to appraise the intruder with curiosity. Opening her eyes, she saw his fervently closed above his flushed cheek, shaming her own detachment. His breath quickened at her ear and his insistence drove her down till her head jammed on the arm of the sofa. Briefly, the motion altered and his tongue turned to bone. His knees slid to the floor and Eleanor pulled free.

Frank curled onto his hunkers, his hand resting

absently on her leg until, fearing offence, he withdrew it. The homage in his eyes discomfited Eleanor. Rising, he brushed his lips at her cheeks in a gesture of thanks.

'Would you like a cup of tea?' He retreated to the kitchenette.

'Yes, please.'

The ringing of cups and spoons accentuated the self-conscious silence. They were in his flat, a two-room basement on Northbrook Road. She thought how odd it must be here in the daytime, eyeing the flip side of the world – the patched soles, pert doggie anuses, pram wheels, the scuttle of leaves and paper. But the subterranean chill gave her the creeps. Trying to feel at ease, she flipped through the sleeves in the album case and pulled out *Tapestry*.

'The record player's broken.' Frank set a tray on the floor in front of the one-bar heater.

'Oh well.' Eleanor returned Carole to her box.

'Milk? Sugar?'

'Both, please.' She settled on the floor and watched the milk spiral to the surface of the tea.

'Tea leaves,' she exclaimed. 'You must be the last person in the world who uses them.'

'I'm a traditionalist.' He grinned. 'Sorry I've no cucumber sandwiches.' His thick fingers dragged open the packet of fig rolls. 'How do they get um-figs into um-fig rolls, Mr Figgerty?' Squatting injun-style, he laughed at the silliness of the old advertisement.

His easy delight jarred her befuddled senses as the silence sweated with the aftermath of their kisses. She blew on her sweet tea and dunked the biscuit. But the flavour of the pap dissolving in her mouth was tainted by the residue of Frank's beer. Absurdly, she wanted to cry. Nothing would taste or be the same again. She was going blindfold down a tight stairway. His touch recalled her, his fingertip tracing a line from her left shoulder to the tip of her crooked middle finger.

'It's cold.'

'It's dead.'

Frank bent his mouth to her fingers and one by one softly sucked each one, his eyes closed, like a baby at the tit. Eleanor squirmed at the sensation of his tongue snailing over her skin.

'I'll bring it back to life,' he said, coming up for air.

She smiled and with her free hand touched the side of his face. 'You're kind, but I'm a lost cause.'

Walking her home, he stopped beneath an almond tree luminous in the night light, and plucked a spray of the nervous blossom to tuck behind her ear. His mouth breathed moistly into hers and retreated. When they turned into her street they heard bath water cascading into a drain. Creamy perfume cloyed in the shrubbery.

Frank sniffed the air. 'Tudor Rose bubble bath.'

'Save the flowers, bath with a friend,' Eleanor laughed.

'I'd like to share a bath with you, Eleanor Leyden.' His hand squeezed hers.

Darkness masked the flush invading her face. 'Me and rubber duckie.'

'Only you,' he whispered.

At the gate his hands cupped her face and his

tongue plumbed her mouth again. She played her own around it, flashing it along the undergroove to tug at its root.

'You have a very professional kiss.' He laughed softly.

Eleanor shrank from this insinuation.

'Good night,' she whispered and ran up the path.

That night the tremors started by Frank's kiss flailed her body. She wanted to throw herself onto a bed of nails, rope her limbs around him, yell till her voice ricocheted down canyons. The idea that he was in love with her capsized her and she shivered with fear.

On Sundays Frank and Eleanor roamed the city, he always shielding her battered left side.

Before them a rectangle of water, framed by shrubs and a narrow path, stretched its peace against the back yards of slipshod terraces where lines of washing saluted the sunset.

'How come you know so many out-of-the-way places?'

'When I moved here I had very little money. So at weekends I treated myself to a bus ride, staying on to the end of the line. Then I walked back to my digs.'

'Did you never get lost?'

'Sometimes. But the city's not that big – in fact it's just an overgrown village. Eventually I'd find my way home.'

'Not very homely, was it?'

'It was all right – except for the holy pictures with creeping eyes and the sodality leaflets the landlady stuck under my door.' Frank's tone grew vehement. 'That was one of the things I was trying to get away from.'

'And have you?'

'I think so, until I go home and find myself doing all the things Mam expects me to do. I was the baby so she mollycoddled me. She was tougher on the girls.'

'Why do you go along with her?'

'Laziness, cowardice.' Frank kicked a stone off the path. 'Maybe if I didn't bounce the ball we wouldn't have any relationship left.'

'I bet she sees through you.'

'She sees what she wants to see. She crochets antimacassars and table runners and tea cosies for my flat. It's like an obsession to cover things. For example, she doesn't see that I'm in love.'

Eleanor yanked away from him. 'Don't say that.'

'I'm not going to hide it.'

'You hardly know me.'

'Love is a gamble.' He laughed. 'I'm a sporting man.'

By now her body was constantly aware of Frank, as though their affection bound their senses together. Occasionally, the recollection of unfinished sex tore at her and she had to force herself to remain seated at her school desk or to join in family meals. When those frenzies had passed, her mind reined back and viewed her lover from a distance. Then she saw a round, ungainly stranger with a piscine expression.

Ronan saw her with the stranger and he quizzed her about him in front of the family. 'Who's Fatso?'

Blushing, Eleanor glowered at her brother. '*Who*?'

'The guy I saw you holding hands with outside Trinity last night.'

'I don't know what you mean.' Her eyes implored him to stop.

Angela, a forkful of lamb at her lips, paused to look from one child to the other, then raised her eyebrows at Dermot.

'I saw you,' Ronan insisted. 'He had froggy eyes. He was carrying a soccer bag.'

'It wasn't me.'

'Oh, sorry. Then it was your twin.'

'Yes.' Eleanor bowed to her plate where her fork chased a pea.

'Nelly's got a boyfriend,' Aoife piped.

'That's enough,' Dermot intervened. 'Leave Eleanor alone.'

It was not long before Angela, certain that the fellow was from the newspaper, pushed her husband to question Eleanor. Dermot was for 'leaving the hare sit'.

'No, no, no,' Angela fulminated. 'She's too young. He's only using her.'

'How the hell do you know?'

'Open your eyes – she's vulnerable, Dermot.'

'And all men are rapists. Is that it?'

'You know perfectly well what I mean.'

'I don't and I don't want to.'

'Then I'm telling her she can't go to Greece unless she stops seeing him.'

'For God's sake, Angela. We don't even know if he exists.'

'She was as red as a beetroot.'

'Well then, going to Greece would be the best thing for her. She'll lose her heart to a handsome fisherman, come home in a swoon, write a few letters and forget about the both of them.'

'It's not her heart I'm worried about.'

Eleanor wished that she did not pity Dermot. As he spoke she watched the veins on his temple pump with a faint blue life, a feature only brought to light by the recent shrinking of his hairline.

'I know that you've been seeing a lot of Frank Mulvey.'

She transferred her attention to the lamppost beyond the rain-heavy garden. The taste of Frank's tongue filled her mouth.

'He's a decent fellow, I know that. But Angela has a point. He's nearly twice your age.'

A crow ratcheting onto the lawn cut Eleanor's gaze. Her eyes met Dermot's.

'So what?'

'So he may expect more than is right or fair from you.'

'I'll keep my legs crossed.'

'I'm being serious, Eleanor. We may have to reconsider your trip to Greece.'

'But you can't.' Anger scorched her eyes. 'I've earned my holiday. That's not fair and you know it's not.'

Dermot shook his head apologetically. 'I'm not going to change my position. You've got around me before but you won't this time.'

'Made you see the truth, you mean.' She flounced to the door. 'You can say what you like but I will see Frank and I will go to Greece.'

Feathered by the rain, she ran down the road. The front gate lazed shut and from the bay window Dermot watched the defiant flame of her hair recede from view.

'Do you think this is his real name?' Louise fanned the book in her lap. 'Comfort. Dr Comfort? It's too good to be true.'

'Louise.' Eleanor dragged at her friend's attention. 'Dermot and Angela are at me about Frank.'

Louise's eyebrows rose. 'I thought they didn't know.'

'Bloody Ronan.' Eleanor pulled a face. 'He saw us at the bus stop. Then went on about it at lunch.'

'I hope you gave him a knee in the balls for that.'

'He's steered clear of me ever since.' Eleanor laughed desperately. 'Anyway, they're saying now that I can't go to Greece.'

'Tell them you've broken it off and sneak out to see him.'

'They'd guess. And what if Ronan saw us again?'

'Then just break it off. There'll be lots of nice fellas in Greece. It's not as if you're madly in love with him.'

'How do you know?'

'Oh, excuse me. Is it wedding bells I hear?' Louise cupped a hand to her ear. 'When am I going to meet him?'

'Shut up. You'd only make a show of me.' Eleanor pouted. 'I know you.'

'OK.' Louise returned to her book.

Relenting, Eleanor crept alongside her friend and considered with her the permutations on foreplay.

Louise's finger alighted on one. 'You could try that with Frank.'

A spasm of desire flushed through Eleanor at the thought of Frank's tongue prising open new spaces in her.

'Mary pretended to be disgusted,' Louise sniggered. 'She said I should burn the book.'

'Have you ever tried it?'

'Not yet.' Louise licked her lips. 'Damien has lovely balls. Like hamsters. What are Frank's like?'

Eleanor bunched up. 'None of your business.'

'I bet he's felt you.'

Eleanor nodded.

'Then the least you can do is feel him back. They don't bite, you know.'

Frank said he would come and visit her in Greece.

'You can't do that.' The protest tumbled out.

'Why not? Do I embarrass you?'

'No.' Eleanor turned away. 'But Louise's parents would be there. I'm in enough trouble already.'

'I'll go incognito. I'll wear dark glasses and a knotted hankie on my head and everyone will think I'm an English tourist.'

'You're mad.'

'No, just a fool for love of you, Eleanor Leyden.'

Doubt lurked in her like a bruise, ignored until something brushed against it. She could love Frank absolutely one moment and the next, chafe to frolic in strange limbs. His love came too easy. It flung up security like a wall.

A week after Eleanor returned from Greece she began to shed her skin. It blistered, then crinkled away like cellophane. She tried to worry off large patches at a time, imagining that she could leave it to dangle in her wardrobe until the fancy took her to wear it again. She recalled the Aegean sun drawing moisture out of her body and how she had wanted to lie naked and watch her body become a new territory, alien and impressive as the electric sea and the tenacious vegetation of that landscape. If she stayed long enough, it would shrivel altogether and leave her a heap of bleached bones waiting to be ground into sand. Louise's father Leo had paraded around the house in his γ-fronts. His soft bulk was punctuated with deep black hair and seemed to fill every room. Eleanor laughed to think what Angela would say if she had seen him cooking with a blue and white apron tied around his bare midriff – 'to keep the fat from spoiling me willie'. She understood why he went undressed. The inescapable glare and heat made even her meagre body seem to swell in voluptuous violence. Beneath the blisters her flesh shone perfect and new.

'Believe it or not,' Angela advised, 'the most soothing thing is cabbage water.'

'I don't want to go around smelling like the Sunday dinner,' Eleanor objected.

'Well, put on this lotion at least, or you'll be scarred.'

The lotion froze through her flesh, chasing the dregs of sunlight from her body.

In the pub with Frank she warmed herself by drinking hot whiskeys. Frank was sheepish at seeing her again.

'I was afraid you might lose your heart to some Greek god.' He grinned.

'They've evaporated.'

'I'm glad.'

She sipped slowly, releasing small mouthfuls down her gullet to savour the spread of the tiny fire through her limbs.

'I see you took to the bottle instead.'

'Yep. I'm piling on the vices.'

'Don't get too fond of it, love.'

'You sound like Angela.' Eleanor shut her eyes. 'I wish people would stop trying to protect me.'

'I'm sorry.' Frank caressed her face. 'It's only that I care.' His hand eased around her neck and his thumb fell to rubbing her nape.

'That's what Angela says, too.' She rolled her head to shirk his hand. 'I can look after myself.'

'Look, Red, I don't know what's eating you but this is pointless. Come on. I'll walk you home.'

'I do have two legs.'

'Suit yourself.'

A tirade boiling in her head, Eleanor ignored the thick rain that pasted her hair to her skull and dribbled along her spine. She turned towards the bakery, and already too wet to care about getting a duck's arse, sat on a stack of pallets. Maybe she could catch a cold and avoid going back to school. That would be mercy. Huddling into her jacket, she lit a damp cigarette. From where she sat she could see the window of her room. She stared up, wondering about the girl who lived there. The girl who should have been there smiled at her, beckoning. A lucky girl. A nice girl. A stranger. The suitcase was still on top of the wardrobe. She should flit and dodge the questions being whetted now about her future.

'What will you be when you grow up?'

'Old and ugly,' was all she could think of to say.

'Bold child. Go to the back of the class.'

'A gravedigger.'

'Over my dead body,' said Dermot.

'A trapeze artist.'

'I give up' – that was Angela.

'A neurosurgeon.'

'You haven't the brains,' Ronan sneered, 'or the hands.'

'A housewife.'

'You'd go mad after three minutes.' Louise knew her through and through.

Suddenly Eleanor laughed. She'd give them something to flap about.

As she rose to go, a light was flung on in the bakery,

opening a pale blue space behind the windows. Passing close to the entrance, she heard the cranking of machines and the greeting of a young man who, with a cigarette cupped in his palm, was eking out the final minutes before his shift began.

'Give us a kiss, love.'

'Some other time.' She walked on.

'Ah, go on. Be nice.'

'Go fuck yourself.'

'Eleanor, what have you done now?' Outrage fevered Angela's cheeks.

'Nothing.'

'Reverend Mother phoned.' Angela waited. 'She says you want to become a nun.'

'Yes.'

'Look at me, please.'

Eleanor half-turned from her desk.

'Why did you say it?'

'Because I wanted to.'

'You'd try the patience of a saint.'

'How would you know?'

'Stop it, Eleanor. Don't think I'm going to turn this one over to Dermot to go soft on you.'

'What are you going to do? Get out the lash?'

'What did you say to Reverend Mother?'

'I told her that God came to me in a dream and I saw myself lying face down on the altar in the chapel and the bishop was cutting my hair with a golden shears and you and Dermot were there. You were crying and you were wearing a white hat.'

'How could you do that?'

'Sorry – would you prefer a pink hat?'

'Don't be cheeky.'

'I don't know what your problem is.'

Angela cast her eyes to the ceiling and took a deep breath. 'I don't believe you have a vocation.'

'Reverend Mother does. She's delighted.'

'*That's* the problem. Have you talked to Ray about this?'

'No. I'm not going for the priesthood.'

'Still, it would be natural to discuss the question of a vocation with him.'

'You can't argue with God.'

Angela put her hands over her ears. 'Stop this at once. We're going to Reverend Mother tomorrow to tell her you want to think this over.'

'I thought you'd be pleased, too.'

'I'm never pleased when you lie.'

Eleanor poked her tongue at the closing door.

'I can't believe you told them that.' Louise shook her head.

'It's all right for you. You know what you want to do.'

'I used to have nightmares about the nuns kidnapping me and turning me into one of them.'

'No fear of that.'

Ignoring the jibe, Louise rummaged for change to pay the bus fare. 'I could eat his little balls,' she said, admiring the wink of the conductor's nates in his shiny-arsed trousers.

Eleanor cocked her head in appraisal.

'Three-plus-six-plus-five-plus-one-plus-four.'
Louise totted the numbers on her friend's bus ticket.
'That's s. What happened to Frank?'

Eleanor shook her head. She could not talk about
him while his letter burnt through her back pocket.

Dear Red,

I regret our silly quarrel, especially because it
spoilt our first meeting after you came home.
You mean so much to me and I was so glad
when you wanted to see me again that I wanted
everything between us to be as if you had never
been away.
I was afraid you might have changed and slipped
away from me. I can't bear not seeing you.

With all my heart,
Frank

His niceness made her feel guilty. She knew she had
been unkind, but she feared his sincerity. She decided
to wait a week, keeping the letter in her pocket. If at
the end of that time it still touched her, she would call
him. If not, she would tear up the sheet of paper and
bury it in the bin. Bye-bye, Frank.

Getting nowhere with the puzzle of s, Louise
turned to her own bus ticket, but when it yielded a
w she snorted. 'So much for numerology. I'll stick to
the stars.'

The post had never been so generous to Eleanor. Apart from Frank's slim missive, fat envelopes fell regularly through the letter box, containing letters for each of the family from Dermot. Based in the US for six weeks to cover the presidential election, he dramatised for them the idiosyncrasies of American life with the tongue-in-cheek style of an innocent abroad. As a postscript to one of Eleanor's letters, he wrote:

> I miss you all very much. Being a 'bachelor' has put me back in touch with some of the old fundamentals. There might even be a book coming on – something to tinker with in my retirement.

And, pen raised again while the confessional mood lingered, another note to say:

> I wish you could see this place. It is so confident. But I'm tiring of the motel bedrooms, every one the same, I wake in the night and wonder have I moved at all.

Eleanor knew that Dermot did not write in this way to Angela. She ripped the letters into tiny squares, her eye momentarily caught by the sight of Dermot nude in a perfunctory motel room. She pushed the image away, as she did the desire which rattled her when he was around. Sex filtered the world for her and danced in her flesh.

The running of the household had changed since Dermot's departure. In the first days it was lopsided and the children were skittish, while Angela looked disconsolate. But when she rallied, there entered an air of martial precision. Assigned his father's chores, Ronan slouched, resentful of everything, even the coal bucket which he filled with bad grace.

'And he has the scowl of Lucifer,' Angela complained when Dermot phoned.

But the man-to-man talk did not improve Ronan's humour.

'She's turning the place into an army camp,' he moaned, and threatened to leave. Later he apologised surlily and kicked the dustbin as he went out the back door.

Because Angela had returned to nursing part-time, the girls were given kitchen duty on certain evenings. Aoife, clutching a Winnie the Pooh cook book, pestered Eleanor to make toffee or honey spice cake.

'See, it's for "Picnics and Expotitions",' she cajoled.

'Expeditions,' Eleanor sighed.

'Pooh says "expotitions".'

'Pooh is a fucking eejit.'

Aoife cried.

'All right,' Eleanor relented. 'Here, show me the page.'

The toffee was like smoked glass. Aoife was intrigued and poked out splinters to suck. 'What happened?'

'I don't know.' Eleanor frowned. 'But I do know that cooking is slave labour.' She would prefer to live out of packets like the treats Dermot sent for Thanksgiving: Betty Crocker, Aunt Jemima and the Sun Maid smiled sweet temptation.

'The fuel of the American dream,' remarked Katherine, who came with Paul and Michael to join the feast.

'Daddy said they eat pineapple with their ham and banana with their chicken over there,' Aoife chirped.

'That's right, pet. And then they spend their life savings getting their teeth overhauled.'

'I think Aoife might need bands,' Angela confided to Katherine.

'Don't be silly. Teeth are part of personality. Next you'll be wanting a nip and tuck.'

Angela gave an embarrassed laugh.

Eleanor sidled up to Katherine.

'How are you doing?' Katherine said in a low voice.

Eleanor twisted her mouth. 'OK, I suppose.'

'Angela giving you a hard time?'

'We don't get on, and with Dermot away she's more bossy.' Eleanor chewed meditatively. 'I can't do a single thing right. I peel too many potatoes, or not enough. I open a new bottle of milk before the old one is finished. She's not that fussy when Dermot is around.'

'I guess she misses him.' Katherine's sigh weighed with her own sorrow for Andrew, who had died during the summer. 'But I do sympathise. Tyranny is often an accumulation of small actions. Angela wants you to know that she is in control.'

'Can I come and stay with you?'

'I'd like that. But it wouldn't be fair on Angela.'

'Please.'

Overlooked by Nostradamus, Eleanor stretched on Tom's bed. The prophet's eyes brimmed with chaos. She grinned, recalling Ronan's jealous expression.

Michael had patted his shoulder and commiserated. 'Soft toenails, old chap.'

Granted a week of freedom, Eleanor enjoyed being a novelty in Katherine's house. She would have liked it even better had Tom been there but he was taking a year out in Germany. She had last seen him at Andrew's funeral when, towering over the throng, he supported his mother's waist with a protective pride that made the woman appear newly frail and vulnerable. Mother and son were bound more keenly than lovers. That day, too, Eleanor saw Katherine undone, crouched at a loss on the edge of the bed in her darkened room, 'what am I going to do? what am I going to do?' spilling from her lips. Beside her, Angela tried to save the bowed woman from utter disintegration. Eleanor stood apart, welcoming

Katherine into the black zone beyond time and will which she had entered already.

Angela gave in to Eleanor out of deference to the bereaved. Seized by a heart attack, Andrew had gone without farewell. For months afterwards Katherine awoke in the deep of night, angrily berating him for that haste. 'Come back, my love, come back,' she called to the emptiness. On hearing this, Tom would come to her room and soothe her until hysteria had drained from her voice. Afterwards, she said, she would lie awake, hugging the radio under the bed-clothes, letting her mind drift with the foreign voices which told her nothing but which seemed to scramble up out of the void. And yes, she confided once to Eleanor, she half-hoped to hear Andrew's neat angli-cised tones come through to her.

'It's good to have another woman in the house.' Katherine beamed when Eleanor joined her in the kitchen. 'You can get very lonesome in a house full of men.'

'Would you have preferred all daughters?'

'No. I couldn't live surrounded by women, either. All that criticising and nit-picking would ate you up.' Her hands made snapping gestures in the air. 'I guess nature got it right. We need the mix.'

'It's kind of weird when you think about it – why women? why men?'

'Because it's fun most of the time.'

'But it's torture, too. Did you ever feel that you were going to have an orgasm in the street?'

Katherine's eyes widened as she shook her head.

'Sex isn't just between people. Anything can start it

off: a colour, a riff of music. It's like another sense, or another dimension to your senses. The funny bit is your body stops being your body when it comes off.'

'I've heard of the multiple orgasm – but the perpetual orgasm? Mmm, tempting.' She stirred her coffee, then suddenly gave a huge sob. 'I'm sorry.' She shook away the tears.

Eleanor sprang to her side and stroked her head.

'It's the aloneness.' Katherine blew her nose loudly into a man's hankie. 'Like stepping outside in winter. You forget how cold it is out there.'

Katherine fought her new loneliness in civil rights campaigns. 'It's not enough,' she said, 'to fight for women's rights only. Women don't want to win freedom at the expense of others. We need to unite the oppressed.'

Eleanor and Louise bowed over the kitchen table, folding leaflets, their sight blurred by the picture of a giant white hand pressing a small black head onto a juicer, above which ran the slogan: DON'T SQUEEZE A SOUTH AFRICAN DRY.

'At the end of the day people look after themselves,' Louise said.

'Not if they believe in social justice.'

'People around here are allergic to anything with the word "social" in it,' Eleanor said. 'They think it means reds under the beds and women train drivers. I wouldn't mind driving a train.'

Louise looked sidelong at her friend. 'I don't think even the Russkies would hire you to drive a train.'

'Shut up.'

'People are afraid of change,' Katherine said. 'They

refuse to see that life is a continual evolution.'

'So Utopia doesn't exist?'

'Utopia is hellishly boring, but looking for it is exciting.'

Eleanor fiddled with her cigarette. Everyone was in a swither looking for something. Why wasn't she? She must be thick or mad. She felt a small click, like a trigger, at the back of her head and pain noosed her skull. She didn't give much for her chances of survival.

Eleanor could not take her eyes from the doubled image of Louise as she posed in front of the mirror, a scarf of Eleanor's tied halterwise over her breasts. The light in Louise's skin made her own pallor seem incomplete, like a plant deprived of the sun.

'Tonight's the night.' Louise twirled and addressed Eleanor through the glass.

'For what?'

'I'm giving myself a birthday present: my first fuck.'

'I thought you had already.'

'Sweet seventeen and never been screwed.' Louise shook her head. 'I'm armed and ready now.' She popped a packet of condoms out of the change pocket in her jeans.

'Good luck.' Eleanor curled tighter on her bed, trying to push away the cramps that bound her belly.

Louise wheedled as she fossicked again in Eleanor's wardrobe and pulled out a suede jacket. 'This is nice.'

'Frank gave it to me.'

'I didn't think he had that much taste.'

'He likes me.'

'I rest my case.' She moved the scarf up around her neck. 'Come to the dance, Nelly-nor. For me.'

'No.'

'Jesus, you're the only person I know who can see politics in a bop.'

'It's not the bop. It's the boppers that bug me.'

'Ah, but how can we know the bopper from the bop?' Louise shimmied the scarf from neck to shoulders to midriff, then swiftly drew it up across her mouth.

Seeing her friend round out her clothes disorientated Eleanor. Whenever she wore them again she would feel that she had borrowed them from Louise – *if* she got to wear them again. The double figure turned and Louise leaned over Eleanor, the suede jacket buttoned across her bare torso, the scarf tied around her neck.

'Can I borrow it for tonight?'

Eleanor sighed. 'I want it back.'

'Of course you'll get it back.'

'Sure. Like the belt and the T-shirt – and the socks.'

'Jesus. Do you keep a notebook of everything you lend? I thought you were a communist – sharing everything.'

'Yeah, well even communists get cold.'

'You're no fun.'

'Oh, take the lot and go.'

'Yeah, I will.'

Eleanor shut her eyes and heard the crackle of static

as Louise brushed her hair, then the sound of clothes being crushed into a plastic bag. Afraid to open her eyes, she sank instead into the shadows of her tightening pain.

Like the return of an exiled leader, Dermot's homecoming was celebrated for a week. Angela opened the party season with Sunday morning drinks. The children were enlisted to serve the guests. Aoife, offering bites to the thronged mouths, cleared a passage for Eleanor and Louise bearing trays of drinks. Down in the kitchen, where he manned the bar, Ronan experimented with cocktails.

'I'm looking for the formula for the perfect leg-opener.' He laughed, handing the girls a shot of pinkish syrup.

'Don't be disgusting,' Eleanor said. 'Anyway, that tastes like cough mixture.'

'Myself and Nelly are working on the recipe for a ball-crusher,' Louise parried.

'Are you a man-hater or what?'

'No, a man-eater.' She grinned fangs at him.

Overhead, their elders grew loud and clung to their glasses, as if to handrails in a rocking train.

'You're not wearing a bra.' A man's voice

assailed Katherine.

'Are you?'

'Ha! But all this back to nature stuff – a bit primitive, isn't it?'

'And you're civilised?'

'Kay, I like you. I only wanted to warn you. People will think you're the merry widow. Mad for it.'

'Go back to your pigsty.'

Flushed with indignation, Katherine swept down to the kitchen and began to fill the kettle. 'Did you hear him?' She turned to the children, who nodded and choked their laughter.

Louise smirked at Ronan and said, 'Why not offer him one of our cocktails?'

Ronan reddened and shook his head.

'They're called ball-crushers.'

Katherine's hooting laugh flew up. 'I'll leave that to you, my dear.'

'OK.' Louise took a glass of Ronan's latest brew and set it on a tray.

'Don't, Louise,' Eleanor hissed. 'There'll be war.' She turned to Ronan for support but he only smiled and folded his arms.

'I'm going to pour it down his trousers.'

'L-o-u-i-s-e.' Eleanor blocked her friend's way. 'Katherine, tell her not to.'

'Eleanor's right, Louise,' Katherine sighed. 'Leave it be. The best thing to do with a creature like that is ignore him.'

'You're all cowards.' Louise put down the tray, and lifting the glass, lowered the drink in one gulp.

Katherine frowned at Ronan's applause. 'I think

you'd better join me in a cup of coffee.'

'I'm fine.' Louise tossed her head and levelled her eyes at Ronan. 'I'll go and collect some empties for refilling.'

The party drained and as midday ebbed into dusk a group of diehard guests drew around the fire.

'Now we have the makings of a good party,' one voice jested and the others fell to dissecting those who had left.

Angela descended to the kitchen to order a tray of coffee and the sandwiches and cake prepared for the inevitable hangers-on. 'They're here for the duration.' She sketched a smile. 'And poor Dermot is dropping.'

'I'll flip the lights and say, "Time now, ladies and gents, time, please",' Ronan offered.

Angela laughed. 'That wouldn't even fizz on them.' Greaseproof paper crackled in her hands. 'No, we'll just have to try and sober them up.'

When Angela was gone Aoife scarpered upstairs, hugging the last bowl of crisps. Louise slumped on a stool while Ronan and Eleanor washed up.

'Give her a cup of strong coffee,' Ronan advised.

But Louise flinched from the sharp brew her friend provided.

'Do you want to lie down?' Eleanor persisted.

'No, I'm OK. Jus', jus' leave me alone.'

Eleanor made a face at Ronan.

'Don't look at me, kiddo. She's a big girl. No one forced her to drink.'

In silence Eleanor resumed her drying.

The standoff was broken by Louise's eruption of hiccups.

'Now she's going to puke,' Eleanor moaned.

'No, she won't. Here, Lou,' Ronan handed her a glass of water – 'drink it backwards.'

'Don't be – stupid –' she hiccupped.

'I'm serious.' Taking her hand, he led her to the sink, and bowing her head, showed her how to gulp from the wrong side of the glass. She giggled and hicced, slewing water around the sink. Ronan's hand moved from her nape to smooth her hair, caressing its flow down her back.

Tinged by jealousy and a lurking sense of betrayal, Eleanor left the room. When she was halfway up the stairs a hand struck out from the gloom and seized her ankle.

'Ouch!' She dropped onto the step.

'Little Nell.' Dermot's voice breathed beside her. 'I haven't seen you all night.'

'It's only six o'clock.'

'This jet lag has me all confused.'

'You should go to bed. No one down there will notice.'

'Too true.' He laughed.

'You're pie-eyed,' she said. 'Come on, I'll help you upstairs.'

'No, no.' Dermot wrenched his arm from her hold. 'I'm not so bad that I can't see one of you where there should be two.'

'I am singular.'

'I know.' His head swung regretfully. 'Tell me, Little Nell, about yourself. Who are you now? What are you? I feel like Rip Van Winkle. That's the trouble with children' – his hand touched her chin – 'puff!

They go. And the space they leave behind is very cold.'

'You wouldn't want us around you for ever.'

'I wish you were flesh of my flesh,' his voice cracked. 'I missed you.'

'We *all* missed you.'

'I suppose so.' His hand waved through the rail to the pleat of light and voices in the hall. 'Angela – this promotion –'. Swiftly his head plunged back to Eleanor. 'You must go to the States. Cut out before it's too late.'

'You're parlatic,' she said.

'Oh Nell, little death knell. Touch me.' He pressed his head into his hands. 'I am cold. I have to tell someone . . .' he sobbed, '. . . to put it away from me.'

She curved her arm around his shoulder. 'All right, all right.'

'One night while I was away' – Dermot raised his head and gulped – 'I was strolling, nowhere in particular, thinking I might stop and have a beer. My foot caught in something soft. I crouched. A man – still warm – blood was running out of his side. He was about my age, black. And the blood went on, taking life with it. Christ.' His head sank again into his hands. 'I thought: I shouldn't be seeing this. It was so intimate. What do you do when a stranger dies in front of you?'

Eleanor stroked Dermot's shoulder.

'I held his hand. I thought, someone has to escort him to the door. But most of all I wanted to run away. I felt sadder for him than for my own father. Then I prayed. The Salve Regina came spilling out of me.

"Eyes of mercy" – whose eyes?' He rounded on Eleanor. 'Mercy, mercy, mercy. It's all nonsense. When I looked at that man I saw the blank space we are falling into. "Banished" is right. You've seen it. I know. You understand.' He rocked and Eleanor swayed gently with him. 'I hear a voice in the night saying, "The next knife is for you."'

'You should go to bed.'

'I'm afraid.'

'I'll read to you.' She smiled.

'I want you, Eleanor. I want you.'

Hot desire wavered between them.

She quickly stood and pressed back against the wall.

'Oh God,' Dermot moaned, 'I'm sorry. So sorry. Sorry.'

Eleanor's voice came from the shadow. 'You've said enough prayers, Dermot.' Sweat chilled on her skin. 'Go.'

In the frost-brittle air of Christmas morning Ray cupped the lambent sea to Eleanor's eye. Her body filled with the water's ease.

'There, do you see him now?' Ray swung the telescope, blurring Poolbeg and the Pigeon House till it picked up a white bird with sooty wingtips. 'A black-headed gull. And those fellows there, see – the red-throated divers – they've likely come down from Scotland or Northern Ireland.'

Again, landmarks skidded away and now three dark birds crested the horizon.

'What brings them here?'

'They get the urge to move' – Ray's hand swung up – 'some birds fly from the South Pole to the North Pole for the fun of it.'

'Maybe they have reasons we don't understand.'

'They don't need reasons.'

Eleanor tracked the creatures pointed at an invisible destiny. Their necks flexed, lofting the pennant heads from the folded bodies, their feathers incandescent under the midwinter sun. She trained her attention on one, whose disdainful eye cut her stare, then tilted and vanished. Cued by this, its companions lifted off the swell, their dark forms staining the sky.

'It's easy for them to move.' She withdrew from the telescope. 'No baggage. I keep a suitcase ready for when I run away – but here I am.'

'Everybody makes flight plans sometime,' he said. 'A psychological escape hatch.'

'Like going on the missions?'

'Possibly.'

Eleanor beamed the telescope on Ray. He feigned a shy simper.

'Go on,' she urged. 'Tell the viewers why you went to darkest Africa.'

Ray watched his toe prise up a loose stone.

'We're waiting.' She gestured to the congress in the bay.

'Yes, it was an escape. I'd be lying if I said otherwise. But I was really in love with God and I wanted to put that to practical use. I didn't want to be a parish priest in some hangar of a church in the suburbs, or some mouldy chapel in the bogs.'

Eleanor laughed. 'You were a snob.'

'I was all of that.' He winced. 'Arrogant. Vain. Oh, I was on the primrose way, all right. But I learnt my lesson. I think that's why they accepted me. They saw that I was too vain to admit defeat and give up. I had to learn to change instead.'

'And now?'

'Now? I don't know.'

'Do you doubt?'

'Sometimes when I get to the South Pole He seems to have moved north.'

'Maybe you'll meet at the equator.'

'There is no equator.'

'Albert Schweitzer. That's what Colm called you.' Ray laughed.

'Margaret argued with him.'

'Margaret always stood up for me. There are days when all I want is just to talk to her for an hour. She was so *clear*.' He hunched again over the telescope.

A shaft of calm lit through Eleanor. She leaned into her mother's shoulder, off-loading the pressure of life.

Ray adjusted the focus on the telescope and swivelled it suddenly. 'Look, look.' He smiled and drew her down beside him. 'Goldeneye ducks. Aren't they beautiful?'

A pair of plump birds jinked on the sea. Broad white spots underscored their eyes. The markings were like great white tears shed by the birds as their masks melted onto their faces.

'They're trapped,' Eleanor said, returning the telescope to Ray. In that movement she glimpsed Frank stepping onto the pier. She looked away, and resting her arms on the parapet, faced the sea and the curve of the city. Beside her Ray was absorbed, making notes in a small book with hard black covers. A gust wisped up his hair. Her hand stretched out to smooth it, then snapped back and delved her pocket for a cigarette. She offered one to Ray. Intent on his notes, he shook his head. Stooping into the wall, she lit the cigarette, drawing deep, eyes shut for the tobacco's dizzying rush. She could feel Frank press close. The hot-fat smell of his breakfast settled around her.

'Hello.' He grinned when she opened her eyes.

'Hi.' She stood up, straightening her jacket.

'So what did you see?'

'We saw red-throated divers which were grey, and goldeneye ducks with white marks under their eyes – I think bird-watchers are colour-blind.' She flung a teasing laugh at her uncle.

Ray shut his notebook with a resolute snap. 'I'll never make an ornithologist of her.'

'Now you know how I feel when I bring her to a rugby match.' Frank laughed in matey exasperation.

'Will we get the Triple Crown next year?'

'Hard to say. There are a few new caps, which should help.'

Eleanor's feet crunched on the path and she refused to halt for Frank's impatient cry. He caught up with her at the footbridge, and dumb with panting, barred her way up the steps.

'There are people trying to come down, Frank,' she said.

He stepped aside, gripping Eleanor's hand before she could flee.

'Come on, Red, don't be silly.' His thumb rubbed the back of her cold spastic hand, trying to revive her affection.

She looked away.

'Oh, Red,' he sighed. 'I chatted to Ray for two minutes – is that so terrible?'

'You know that's not the point,' she said without facing him.

'All right, all right, I'm sorry I fell into the old

man-to-man trap.'

'It's hopeless, isn't it, Frank?' She swung to challenge him.

'What? I try, Eleanor. Compared to some fellows, I'm not bad at all.'

'I don't mean that. I mean we argue more than we talk now, don't we?'

'Ah, Red, don't start this. Not on Christmas Day. I'll do anything to make you happy. You know that.'

She forced a smile. 'It's not your fault, Frank. It's –'

'Please' – his hand shot out to stop her words – 'I only have half an hour before I go to my sister's house. Let's leave the soul-searching for today and just be nice to each other.' He pulled a doleful face.

'OK.' She tucked her arm under his. Today, today, today, she thought, always a reason not to talk. From the top of the bridge she looked back along the pier to where Ray stood bowed at the telescope, as if funnelling himself into another element. 'I need clarification too, Ray,' she muttered.

From the corner of the common room Leonard Cohen assuaged the girls' soulful hankerings as Maureen, laying out tarot cards, professed to see into their romantic fates. Eleanor shuddered at the certainty of those lies and the fervour of her classmates' faith in them. The cards, the horoscopes, the bus ticket numbers, the black cats – all promised a Messiah who, opening their legs, would transform the girls' lives. The only card she wanted to see was the hanged man. She withdrew from the group before her turn came and crawled under the table in the corner. She crouched, hooping her arms around her legs and pressing her face against her knees to see how small she could make herself. She hummed softly, out of tune with the record.

'Nelly's scared of the future,' Louise taunted.

Eleanor ignored the jibe, but could not push away the dread that there might be forces out there against which she was powerless. Broken glass cascaded across her shoulder. She pressed her face tighter to her knees, hugging the pain, until a galaxy of sparks flew through her head.

'Let me guess . . .' Louise's voice broke through the aeons. '. . . you're a beetle.'

'No, I'm a pebble.'

'You're a fucking fruitcake.' Louise sat on the table and swung her legs, thumping her heels into Eleanor's ribs. Eleanor unrolled and stretched on her stomach. 'I've made a decision.'

'Oh?'

'I'm going to carve headstones.'

Louise snorted. 'How do you think of the things?'

'Genius.'

'Have you told Derm and Angie Baby?'

'I've only just thought of it.' Eleanor stood, drawing level with Louise. 'Don't tell anyone. I don't want a fuss like the last time.'

'You're serious about this?'

'Yep.'

'Got you.' Louise winked. 'But I'd love to be a pimple on your arse when you tell them.'

She'd be a long time waiting to be scratched, thought Eleanor that evening. The scuffed suitcase and its hoard gaped at her feet, a displaced object. The honeymooners who had carried it to the Isle of Man were strangers. She should have run away years ago. Crushed glass rained down with the sound of rattling chains, filling and overflowing the cardboard sides, drowning the cries that wrenched her heart. She wanted to dive through the glass and never surface. She kicked over the lid, snapped home its fasteners, and lugged it downstairs to the back passage, where she propped it against the bins.

While she doodled on the door of the toilet stall, Eleanor overheard a bitch-in.

'I could kill ~~Louise Makarios~~' – that was Maureen. 'She thinks she's the bee's fucking knees just because she doesn't have to do Irish.'

'I don't know how she got out of it,' Julie said.

Eleanor crouched attentive, the red marker still poised between her fingers.

'Because greaseball Daddy supplies the altar wine cheap,' Maureen sneered. 'And it's poison. I took a swig one day and I nearly puked.'

'Poor Father Ryan.'

'He wouldn't know if it was petrol he was drinking.'

'That might do him some good.'

'And the way she flirts with anything in trousers – even Father Ryan.'

Striding from the stall, Eleanor swung her fist at Maureen. Caught off balance, Maureen toppled to the floor, thumping her jaw against the rim of the hand basin on her way down. When she yelled, blood spouted from her mouth and sprinkled the grey lino.

'You bitch!' Julie spun to face Eleanor, who grabbed her ponytail, tugged it hard, and flung her onto the bleeding Maureen. With a huge gust of laughter she fled the loos and pelted back to the classroom.

Angela insisted that Dermot be stern. She stood like a warden at the door while Eleanor preceded him into the living room.

Dermot shut his eyes before he spoke. 'You've gone too far this time, way too far.'

Eleanor waited.

'Have you nothing to say?'

She grinned. 'It's like *Hawaii Five-O*: anything I say may be taken down in evidence and used, blah blah blah . . .'

'Don't you realise how serious this is?'

'What do you want me to say?'

'That you regret what you did.'

'I'd be lying.'

'You are beyond me.'

Eleanor was sullen.

'I won't waste my time trying to reason with you.' Dermot inspected his fingernails. 'Mother Noonan wants to suspend you for the rest of the term. Angela and I have agreed that you are to go and stay with her parents –'

'What about my Leaving?'

'Listen to me.'

Eleanor clenched her jaw.

'You'll work in the hotel for a few hours every day. The rest of the time you can study. The teachers will set reading and exercises. You can send the exercises in every week. You will not contact Louise or anyone else while you are there. Understood?'

'Yes, commandant.'

The Deerview Lodge was between seasons when Eleanor arrived. The wooded valley loured under a mizzle which hung clouds over the hill tops and clagged the windows. Damp penetrated the walls and curled off shrouded furniture in the desolate lounges. The dining-room tables and chairs were stacked to one side, exposing the motley stain and fray of the carpet. The Tighes were listless. Syl's expectorations rattled through the hall. His wife sat in her office, teapot at her elbow, red veins breaking on her cheeks.

She turned an offended expression on Eleanor. 'I knew that one was a bad influence on you.' She flapped her hand dismissively. 'Your granddaddy'll tell you what to do.'

'He's not my granddaddy.'

Mrs Tighe's head dropped over a mess of brown envelopes and receipt books. 'I'm too busy to argue with you. Go and talk to Syl.'

Eleanor lugged her bags up to the small bedroom at the back of the annexe. The beds were unmade, their mattresses watermarked by the emissions of strangers. She trailed through the ghostly corridors and found Syl studying the racing form in the bar.

'Ha!' He waved his cigarette as she approached. 'Here's one for you: Devil's Advocate. A filly, too.'

'I don't bet.'

'Oh, very prim. But you blotted your copybook all the same.' He slid off the stool. 'Come on, Roger, let's show the girl her duties.' The retriever lumbered upright and padded behind them into the hall.

'You'll start by cleaning all the windows.' The old man gestured at the sun porch lined with window boxes of plastic plants. 'You could wipe those yokes, too. Then work your way up to the bedrooms. After the windows there's the hoovering, dusting, the ladies and the gents to do. Betty will be in next week to help.'

'Thanks.'

Opening business was desultory at the hotel. Occasional windswept groups of Sunday drivers came in, rubbing their hands and ordering tea and biscuits. Eleanor was sent to prepare the trays, and under winking warnings from Syl was directed to ask *him*, not his wife, to carry them into the bar. Mrs Tighe sucked a peppermint before emerging from the office to parse the weather with the guests. Betty came on weekdays to cook lunches and a boy named Teddy helped in the bar and dining room. Once or twice an overnight visitor came, a salesman or a misguided tourist, whose expressions tweaked at the odour of damp and the sight of the porridgy beds.

Bar trade picked up on Friday and Saturday nights. One Saturday morning Teddy breezed into the gents to find Eleanor blanched in dismay at the vomit splattered on the floor and clogging the urinals, and the explosions of shit crusting the toilet bowls. He took her by the shoulders and steered her out of the midden. Having settled her in a chair in the lounge, he vanished and reappeared with a cup of sugary tea.

'That's where all their money ends up,' he laughed.

Eleanor's face curled as she sipped the tea.

'If it's any help, in future I'll do the gents and you can do the ladies.'

'Thanks, Teddy.' She patted his arm. 'I doubt that the ladies will be much better, but I'll do it. Syl will tell me it's rounding off my education.'

'I was going to ask you to come out for a drink some night, but you'll likely not be tempted now.'

Eleanor grinned. 'I don't mind, except that I'm gated.'

'What's that?'

'I'm not allowed out.'

'They can't keep you under house arrest.'

'They can.'

'Look, next Thursday, when they go to the golf club, I'll send my brother up to do the bar and we can go out.'

'That'd be nice. Thanks.'

In the afternoons she tried to study, making her desk at the dressing table in one of the hotel bedrooms. She draped the invasive mirror with a blanket. The mirror read the back of her mind. Before she let the blanket drop she pressed her face close to the glass, trying to see what lay behind her eyes, but the shutters were down, hiding the things she didn't want to see. For the same reason she had beat up Maureen and Julie. She hated the truth their words echoed in her. A blank. Hugging a hot-water bottle to her waist, she bent over her books. The mystical importance pressed on them in the class-room dissolved here and the teachers' voices dimmed in her ears. She flipped the pages back and forth, trying to find a heading or an illustration that hooked her inter-est, but the words were inert. She looked at the essay questions set for her but these, too, were as impenetrable as another language. Her effort was baffled by the fact that she recognised the words but their connections evaded her. She prowled the room, rested her head against the window, ever waiting to see a deer. Nothing moved in the landscape save the drifts of rain sharpening the greens and purples of the hillside and the odd rook protesting over the trees. Out here time stagnated, the days seeping imperceptibly into one another.

She returned to the dressing table, and scowling with frustration, opened and slammed its drawers. Something rolled in the middle drawer and she paused to lift out the bottle of little green pills. Mogadon. She recognised the dope from Dermot's bathroom cup-board, the panacea for his 'tossy' nights. She rattled them like a tube of sweets. What if she ate them?

She lifted the blanket off the mirror and stared at her face. The eyes regarded her impassively. The sight of her own features could surprise her. Most of the time she forgot what she looked like, then, caught un-awares, she found a half-familiar face watching her, as though she were a stranger. Now her face oscillated like a shrink's trick picture, the candlestick grasped, then vanished, between two profiles, Eleanor's face split and peeled away to reveal its replica, and again and again without diminishing or disappearing.

She proposed the bottle to the face in the glass. The head swung. She opened the bottle: fifteen little green demons. Would that be enough to kill? Or would they merely sicken her? She imagined the wee-waw of the ambulance and the horror of the stomach pump. She poured the pills into her hand and closed her eyes, braced for the glide into abnegation. She clamped them in her mouth and began to chew. They tasted like poison. She chuckled inwardly. Her last little joke. Her eyes flashed open and she forced a Cheshire grin, the mush of green and white bubbling at the corners of her mouth.

The eyes in the mirror were not part of the grin. They told her she was a fraud. She nodded, and lifting up the wastepaper basket, spat the masticated pills into it. She spat several times and hawked to dredge up any swallowed fragments, streels of spittle draping the cigarette-scarred plastic. After she could spit no more she threw the empty bottle in, thinking that that would make a tale for the next guest to unravel. When she stood up her head lurched giddily. With a drunkard's deliberation she piled the books and the hot-water bottle against her chest and willed her feet, step by step, to carry her to the door.

'At your service, ma'am.' Teddy mock-doffed and held the bicycle steady while Eleanor settled on the cross-bar.

Roosted there against his chest, she gasped in the freewheel swoop between shadow-swollen hedge-rows.

'The Devil's Glen,' Teddy said when the bike crossed a small bridge over a frantic stream and helter-skeltered through a mob of trees.

'Spooky.' Eleanor huddled closer.

'We'll likely see himself on the way back. His eyes are like red lamps, they say.'

'How *will* we get back up?'

'You can sit on the bike and I'll push you,' Teddy joked.

In the pub he raised his pint to hers. 'Here's to liberation.'

'Three cheers.' She relished the first bitter taste of the beer. 'It really does seem like getting out of prison. You forget how the world feels.'

'You call this the world' – he panned the smokey room and its scatter of murmuring regulars.

Her face puckered. 'It's better than the Colditz up the road.'

'Well, I've had my fill of it.' The boy shook his head. 'I'm saving for Amerikay.'

'What'll you do there?'

'I've heard there's work going in Atlantic City. That's the place. You can make a packet on the building sites.'

'Will you come back?'

'I don't know.' He pondered. 'Depends. I seen fellows come back and they might as well never've been away. They said they didn't like the life. But the way I look at it, they never gave it a chance. I'll only come back if things can be different.'

'How different?'

'If I have the money to start my own business.' He swigged his beer. 'I'm not coming back to clean old Tighe's jacks.'

They laughed together and fleetingly Eleanor regretted that this boy was leaving.

'What about you?'

'Yeah. I suppose I'd like to get out too – but I've no plans.'

'You're doing the Leaving, aren't you?'

'So they tell me.'

'Won't your folks want you to go to college? Be a teacher or something?'

'Some hope.' She ground out her cigarette. 'Let me buy you another drink – and is it OK if I make a quick phone call?'

'Do they bug the phones up there?' Teddy arched his eyebrows.

'All but.'

The jangle of the coins in the box startled her into wonder at herself. Only when the receiving voice said 'news room' twice did she press button A. She could tell that Frank was bemused by her call. They chatted until she heard her money running out and at the last minute she announced: 'Frank, I'm not going to sit the Leaving.'

Teddy was staring into his pint.

'Sorry.' She slid in beside him. 'It was like getting through to the moon.'

His mouth flexed a tolerant smile. 'Boyfriend?'

'Sort of.'

'Is he lonely?'

'We didn't get around to that. He's a journalist. He's going to encode messages to me in his copy.'

'Sounds tricky.' Fixing his eyes on her, he drained his glass. 'I think you're a girl that spells trouble.'

She did not respond.

'Will we go?'

She looked at her half-finished drink. 'If you like.'

In silence they walked back up the hill, Teddy pushing the bike. When they reached the Devil's Glen Eleanor tightened her jacket across her chest. The trees patrolled the darkness, and strenuous with the wind, resisted the stream's interminable plunder. She flinched when Teddy took her twisted hand, then, easing, let him hold it. Neither spoke until they had quit the glen.

'No bogeyman.' He laughed.

'The spooks are in our heads.'

'I suppose so.'

Suddenly Teddy began to sing and the rising timbre of his voice alleviated the night's oppression. 'Dance, dance, wherever you may be' – the call grew around the boy and girl – 'I am the Lord of the Dance, said he . . .' it rang out '. . . and they cut me down and I leapt up high, for I am the dance that will never, never die.' Believing it, he sustained the song until they reached the hotel gate.

'Better shut up now.' He laughed, shy of himself.

'I enjoyed that, Teddy.' Eleanor brushed her lips to his cheek but his mouth swerved, and catching hers, his tongue skittered across her teeth.

'See you tomorrow.' He swung onto the bike and pedalled quickly into the blackness.

Eleanor surprised Angela and Dermot by saying that she wanted to go to the school debs' ball.

'That's what I call having your cake and eating it.' Angela shook an exasperated look at the girl.

'So what, if I can get away with it?'

'Oh, let her, Mummy.' Aoife glowed.

'I won't stop you,' Angela said. 'But we'll have to talk to Mother Noonan.'

'Sister, you're supposed to call her now.'

After serving her time at the Deerview Lodge, Eleanor had refused to go back to school. Contrary to Louise's foreboding, Dermot did not oppose her intention of becoming a stonemason, but insisted that she sit the Leaving first.

'I'm done fighting with you, Eleanor,' he said. 'And this is the last thing I will push you to do. Be a stonemason, be a gravedigger, fly a kite, anything you like *after* you've done the Leaving.'

It was Angela who made the practical objections. 'That's heavy work,' she said, 'man's work. And

with your poor arm I don't see how you'll be fit
for it.'

The disfigured arm was to draw up more old frictions
between Eleanor and Angela. Granted permission to
'come out' with her former classmates, Eleanor set to
plotting the night's debauchery with Louise and
discussed her dress with Angela and Katherine.

'I'm not wearing white, that's for sure,' she said.

'But it's traditional, love,' Angela cajoled.

'I'd feel like Hark the Herald Angel.'

Katherine laughed. 'A misbegotten angel.'

'I'm going to wear white,' said Aoife. 'A lovely
white dress with a long tail.'

'Train.'

'Tail.'

'You're not a doggie.'

'Stop it.' Angela rapped her knuckles on the table.

Finally Eleanor borrowed a green Kashmiri robe
from Katherine, whose wardrobe was a bazaar of
fabrics, scented with sandalwood. She chose Stavvy
as her partner.

'You're not bringing *him*.' Louise's face wrinkled.

'But I like him.'

'Yeah, but you don't fancy him. And I don't want
my baby brother hanging around me all night.'

'He'll be hanging around me. Anyway, I've already
asked him.'

'Well, unask him.'

'No.'

Frank tore his beer mat into tiny strips when Eleanor

told him about the ball.

'I'll make it up to you,' she said.

'Great.'

'You know Dermot would freak if I brought you.'

'It's about time Dermot copped himself on.'

'Look, it's for your sake. He could make things difficult at work.'

'I can handle that. I'm just sick of this hole-and-corner business.'

'Sorry. How about a bit of other business?' She licked his ear.

His hands moved across her back in half-hearted surrender.

The row erupted between Angela and Eleanor on the evening of the ball. Angela came to her room, bearing a faded grey leather ring box.

'I kept it especially for your coming out.' She handed the box to Eleanor. 'It belonged to your mother.'

Eleanor contemplated the white gold band crowned with a ruby encircled by seed pearls.

'I don't remember it.'

'I thought it might have been an heirloom but Ray said not. Your father must have given it to her.'

'Or someone else.'

Angela smiled. 'Maybe. He must have been very fond of her. It's charming. And it's just your colouring.'

Eleanor frowned at the ring. She was displaced by the cluster of gems surfacing from a life unconnected with hers. The mother she remembered slid out of her ken.

'It should have been buried,' she said.

'You can't put it there.' Angela's cry jolted Eleanor back into herself.

'Why not?'

'Because . . . because it's unlucky.'

'Old wives' tales,' Eleanor scoffed.

'Besides, it doesn't – I mean it would look nicer on your other hand.'

'What you mean,' Eleanor said, continuing to twist the band onto the middle finger of her bent left hand, 'is that it draws attention to my deformed arm, which I should be trying to hide because it makes you and other people uncomfortable.'

'No, no.' Angela blushed.

'Yes, Angela, yes. All my life you've been trying to make me hide it, mask it, pretend that it doesn't exist. Well it does.'

The colour left Angela's face. 'All right, Eleanor, all right,' she sighed. 'Put the ring on that finger. Forget about the cape Dermot and I gave you. Go naked, for all I care. I've tried to love you. I've tried to protect you. We wanted to give you every chance but all you do is throw it back at us. Goodbye, Eleanor. From tonight I do not know you.' Pressing a hankie to her mouth, she left the room.

Aoife peered around the door. 'Daddy says are you ready to come downstairs for your champagne?'

'Yes, Pixie,' Eleanor said. 'Take my hand.'

A shaft of pure cold sliced Eleanor. She reached for warmth in the child's trust but the cold gripped and she parted from the self who descended automatically to the bright room. She saw Dermot move forward in an embrace.

Ronan winked. 'You look good, sis.' He handed
her a flute of champagne.

'Is Angela coming down?' Dermot fidgeted.

'She ran into her room,' said Aoife.

Eleanor squeezed the child's hand before she could
say more. 'Why don't you call her again, Pixie?' she
suggested.

'Your beau is late.' Dermot checked his watch for
the third time.

'You should keep the dress,' Katherine said.

'I couldn't.'

'Do, it becomes you.'

Biting her lip, Eleanor looked at the faces surround-
ing her. Their smiles were for a daughter–sister–niece
they had created. She balked at her own duplicity and
havered in regret for their kindness, but already the
alcohol was misting her senses.

Before the dancing began the debutantes and their
partners lined up to be presented to the alumni com-
mittee and to receive a gift to launch them on the
world.

'It's like a wedding march,' Stavvy whispered to
Eleanor.

'A pair of tights!' Louise exclaimed, pulling open
her package. 'Now what's the significance of that?'

'They should have given you a pair of crotchless
knickers,' said Damien.

'Or a bottle of mace,' quipped Eleanor.

The band laboured into a cover of 'Thank Heaven
for Little Girls'.

Stavvy winced.

'Pity Sambo didn't bring his bongo drums,' said a boy with drooping eyes, and pointed to a table on the facing balcony. There a lean black youth bent to light his cigarette from a candle, his free hand protecting the opera scarf that draped his neck.

'Mmmm.' Louise approved.

'I wonder if he has any juicy sisters?' The droop-eyed boy winked at Damien. 'They're bad girls.'

'Fuck off.' Eleanor flashed. 'You sexist, racist pig.' She flung a glass of red wine over his rented shirt.

'Cow!' He quivered.

'Come on, Stavvy. Let's dance.'

'Anything you say.' Stavvy grinned.

The band was doing its best to rock and roll.

'How do they manage to make Elvis Presley sound like Frank Sinatra with a head cold?' Stavvy shouted as he caught Eleanor's hand on a turn. 'Poor Elvis. RIP.'

'I didn't know you could dance.' Eleanor smiled.

'Why did you ask me, then?'

'Because I like you, I suppose.'

'Shove over, kiddo.' With a side swipe of her bum, Louise knocked Stavvy out of time.

Eleanor slid between them. 'Piss off, Louise.'

Back at their deserted table, Stavvy inspected a half-empty glass. 'Was this mine?' He drained it, then shook his head. 'No – maybe it was this one.'

When he began on his fourth glass Eleanor seized his arm. 'Stop, Stavvy. You'll make yourself sick.'

'Leave me alone.' He jerked away. 'You're as bad as her.'

'That's not fair, Stavvy. I brought you to this dance.' She shut her eyes and withdrew to the cold space at her core. 'Do you really want to go home?' she asked from behind her closed face.

'No.' He pouted.

'All right.' She gathered herself again for the effort of involvement. 'Let's go and find the party.'

They were two hours getting to Julie's party. Damien, who had borrowed his mother's car for the evening, diverted to a friend's flat where he could score some draw. Parked beside the canal, they filled the Renault 4 with the herbal smoke which sent them all into collapsing giggles.

'Pigs in space,' drawled Damien, and Louise, echoing him, sank into another fit of giggles that raked her gold headband over one eye.

'What'll your mammy say when she gets a whiff of this in the morning?' she gasped.

Damien shook his head, holding down the smoke, then said through its dragon belch, 'I'll tell her it was your perfume and she'll get so happy with the whiff, she won't mind.'

'It's like being inside a bong.'

They giggled again and Eleanor sang: 'Time to fly, little piggies.'

Once out of the gassy steamer, she felt the laughter fall away. Bending a polite smile at Julie's parents, who sat drinking coffee in their kitchen (no sign of Aunt Trish), she passed through to the party room, where she gulped a glass of wine and tucked herself into the corner of a sofa. Stavvy followed, his face now hung with melancholy. He flopped beside her.

'Dance if you like, Stavvy,' she said. 'I'm just sitting out for a while.'

He declined. 'I need to rest too.'

'OK.'

'I wish, I wish ...' he mumbled, '... I wish you were my sister.'

'You probably wouldn't like me if I was.'

'Do you like Ronan?'

'Most of the time. But most of the time he doesn't like me.' She pursed her lips. 'I think he prefers Louise.'

'Let's do a swap.' Stavvy brightened, then, arrested by a loud burp, vomited plethorically into Eleanor's lap. He stared in amazement at what he had done.

The fluid seeped warmly over Eleanor's thighs and she blocked her nose against the steaming reek. 'Fuck you, Stavvy,' she groaned, trying to stand and hold the dress without spilling the puke.

'Sorry, sorry.' He jigged uselessly. 'It was the chicken fricassee.'

'Stavvy, don't be an ape. Find the loo.'

'You can't bring him anywhere.' Louise shook her head over Eleanor's effort to rinse the dress in a hand basin. 'Here, spray some of this on it.' She lifted a can of air freshener off the cistern. 'You'll smell like a butterfly.'

'Butterflies don't smell,' Eleanor said. 'Anyway, I'm going home.'

'Well, take Stavvy with you and dump him somewhere.'

'Don't worry, Cleopatra. He won't spoil your night.'

As good as her word, Eleanor offered to compensate Frank for missing the debs' ball.

'Come to bed with me,' she said.

'What? Now?'

'Yeah. Catch it while it's hot,' she laughed.

'But . . . oh God, Eleanor . . .' He sweated. 'Are you serious?'

'Yes, relax.' She moved onto his knee. 'You don't have to. I just thought it might be fun.' Her fingers tripped around the belt of his trousers.

'Yes,' he croaked. 'Is it all right? Are you –?'

'I'm insured.' She grinned.

'You're very organised.' Resentment snuck into his tone.

'Men!'

'Forgive me.' He caught her hand and kissed it. 'You surprised me. You make it so easy.'

'What did you want to do? Beat me into submission?'

'No, my darling.' He stood, still holding her hand,

and led her behind the curtain that screened his bedroom.

'Thank you, Eleanor, thank you.' His gratitude slumped beside her, one arm strapped across her chest.

She patted his buttock reassuringly.

'Do you want a towel?' He opened one eye up at her.

'No, thanks.' She shook her head. 'I'm going to the bathroom.'

In the mirror she watched her hands cup her breasts, wondering how they felt to a stranger, and played her mind back over her romp with Frank. It had taken all her strength not to laugh when, after coy nibbling at her nipples, he had pushed into her and shaken himself empty with frantic urgency, until he fell away, spent, the loving accomplished in moments.

She laughed now. Dear, how she laughed, sitting on the edge of the bath, her blood starting up when she turned the faucet and the flame leapt in the geezer. Softening in the deep, hot water, she rinsed off Frank's milky overspill, and parting the lips that he had bruised, reached into the point where her laughter expanded to a crow of delight.

Frank was not the only one whom Eleanor embraced. Robbie was in first med with Louise, although for him it was the third time around.

'Like a hamster on his wee wheel.' He laughed, heedless of the fact that this was his last chance to get the exams. Putting himself through college, he saved on rent by squatting. When Eleanor met him he was snug in the cellars under the college theatre. Their encounters on the horsehair mattress were paced by the stamp of feet and histrionic declamation on the stage above.

At the burst of applause, Robbie sprang up and bowed, gesturing to his erect penis. 'Johnny Rotten salutes you.' Then he flopped on top of her.

Eleanoar hugged him. 'You should be up there.'

'Och, I joined in my first year. Joined everything, in fact, wide-eyed little fresher that I was. But that lot took theirselves too seriously: all Oliviers in embryo. They said I was too much of a one-man band. Aye. In the sash my father wore and all.' He sat bolt upright, his thin, hairless chest white as a child's. 'So, aren't you the lucky one to have me here all to yourself,' he chirped.

'I am.' Eleanor smiled, running her finger down his spine.

'Now you've woken wee Johnny again.' He laughed, diving under the rough blanket to tickle her open with his tongue.

'You're great,' he whispered hotly when they came off together.

'You're not so bad yourself,' she said, kissing the exhausted Johnny Rotten.

On nights when she stayed out altogether she told Angela and Dermot that she was with Louise. But Louise herself now rarely slept at home. Everything was over between her parents and she did not want to see the hole in their lives.

'I hate it.' She shuddered. 'Leo stares at the TV all

night and Stavvy stays in his room, wanking or something, while Mother is out gallivanting. And the place is like a tip since Mary left.'

'Doesn't Leo mind?'

'Of course he minds. He pretends not to, says he doesn't like parties.'

'But he used to.'

'I know that.' Louise twitched impatiently. 'It's her friends he doesn't like. All he wants is her there.'

'Poor Leo.'

'He's pathetic. When she is there he's so happy. He's like a fucking doormat with a welcome grin, waiting to be walked all over.'

'Why don't they move back to Greece? He'd have her to himself there.' Eleanor recalled Mr Makarios's carefree manner in their holiday villa.

Louise snorted. 'She wouldn't go. Full stop. When I said he should go anyway, he went mad and said he doesn't belong there any more. This is his home, he said.'

'But his plot of land?'

'He calls that his "dreamspace". When he's in a good mood he designs houses for it with swimming pools and olive groves and beehives. If you ask me, he'll only need a six-foot box by the time he gets there.'

'That's a shame. It sounds nice.'

'Don't I know!'

For Eleanor, too, home, now, was scarcely home. Since her debs' night she had arrived at a tacit accommodation with her foster parents, giving them sketchy accounts of her comings and goings, which they did not challenge. She saved part of her newspaper earnings for her stonemasonry apprenticeship and gave Angela a sum towards her upkeep. Occasionally, when she looked at Dermot's face furrowing with age, she grew wistful for their old sparring comradeship, but wary of its implicit danger, she knew that it was better dead.

By a curious reversal she began to like Angela, as if their mutual release from dutiful affection cleared the way to friendship. Yet she hung back, uncertain how that amity might be established. With Ronan she had reached an easy alliance. Each respecting the other's secret life, they coincided in the small hours to brew coffee and to talk.

'Blue Mountain.' Ronan wiggled his nose over the acrid beans. 'Have you ever wondered how many mountains are called Blue Mountain?'

'No.' Eleanor yawned. 'I count sheep instead.'

'Seriously though' — the boy's eyes rounded — 'people talk about the forty shades of green, but think about blue.'

Eleanor shut her eyes. 'No go. All I'm getting is black.'

'Change the channel,' he ran on. 'What I'm saying is, that blue is a feeling. You get "the blues". It's music, it's mood. Everyone has a postcard of "The Blue Guitar". And there's blue blood, the divine right of kings.' He paced the kitchen, ignoring the steam blowing from the kettle. 'I wouldn't be surprised if God is blue.'

'Maybe you should stick to French Roast, Ronan.' Eleanor peered at him. 'Or are you stoned?'

'Shit.' He sprang across the kitchen to switch off the kettle. 'That'll get rid of the blackheads.' He wiped his face and glasses with a tea towel. 'Speaking of which, I see Lulabelle in college. Well, in the Buttery.'

'So you're both swotting hard.'

'Yeah, well, I have to greet my public. But she's heading for deep shit. First med is a weeder.'

'Are you her mentor?'

'Fuck off.' Ronan blushed. 'Just telling you that your friend is —'

'Blue?'

'She's blue, all right.' He giggled.

Sensing a subterfuge, Eleanor felt a riff of anger in her blood. 'Louise knows how to look after herself.'

'I hope so.'

One month later Eleanor took fright at a ghostly inward stirring and the absence of blood, but when she was certain that no child was being fleshed in her womb, she fancied that the sensation was a new identity forming in her. She decided to name it with a title empty of expectation. She told the stonemason her name was Lilac.

'You won't smell so sweet after a day in here,' he warned, his quick eye perusing her. 'You'll need overalls and gloves. You're the first girl we've taken on, so you'll have to bear with us.'

Bill was the third stonemason Eleanor had approached and after stubborn argument from her he had agreed to give her a six-month trial at half-pay. 'You only have one arm,' he said with finality.

They toured the yard and the workshop, breasting the gritty air. Slabs of stone leaned haphazardly against the walls, some carved and polished, like envelopes waiting to be addressed, others still rough from the quarry. She rested her hand on a frayed pink edge.

'We get that in from Italy,' Bill said. 'High-class stuff – if you want to rest in style.'

But Eleanor was watching the shadow of a child expecting a message in the lines of her parents' headstone.

'... nearly too good for graves,' her boss continued. 'I'm thinking of branching into fireplaces. Then I can call the place Hearth to Earth.' He chuckled. 'Over here is our heavenly host.'

Materialising in the workshop's gloom, angels knelt with folded wings and bowed, sorrowful faces. Eleanor caressed the wings of one, and recalling the flutter of a snow angel, heard the echo of her parents' voices calling her to follow them. She snatched her hand away as if it was burnt, half-expecting the plumage to flare and rise.

'People worship statues,' she reflected.

'They're going for plain slabs these days, I can't shift that crew' – a flick of his hand dismissed the angels. 'Now I think it's time for a sup of tea.'

The stonemason's assistant, ashen with dust, leaned out of the prefab hut to inspect the newcomer.

'Jarlath, this is Lilac.'

'Hi.' She grinned and shook his hand.

'Have you got a sister?' Jarlath tilted his head, his smile showing a jaunty gap between his teeth.

'Don't say I didn't warn you.' The boss ushered her to a plastic bucket seat.

Thin Lizzy whackfalthedaddioed from a radio-cassette player. Eleanor's eyes strayed to a surreptitious frieze of girlie cutouts above the window of the cabin.

'You can have a corner for Robert Redford.'

Jarlath's eyes followed hers.

'Thanks,' she said, 'but he's not my hero.'

'Who are you into?'

'I've no big favourites.' She considered for a moment. 'I like Sid Vicious and Patti Smith.'

'A mad woman.'

'The Snotpickers.'

'Gerrup the yard.'

'I hate to disturb you.' Bill stood and shot his tea dregs out the door. 'But get back to work,' he rounded on them.

'Yessir, Major Hawkeye. Sir.' Jarlath sprang to attention, then nudged Eleanor. 'He's all right, really. As long as you do your work. And no messing on the job.'

'I'll remember that. Thanks.'

The next day, for the gas, she tacked up a picture of the pope between two fantasy women and stepped back to scan the frieze. She felt no kinship with these silicone dreams but their faces seemed to jeer her puniness and girlish naiveté. They were queens of sex, and envy of their smooth prowess ticked deep inside her.

'So you like the little pictures, Lilac?' Bill's voice nuzzled her ear and his belly closed against the small of her back, hazing her into an aroused confusion.

'Yes ... I mean no ... I was just looking,' she gabbled, unwilling to face him.

'Jarlath will be glad,' he said and pulled away. 'Some day I expect to go out there and find him carving Raquel Welch.'

Eleanor stepped back from the pictures but could

not meet the boss's eyes, knowing that his laugh was on her. 'Excuse me,' she said and dodged to the loo, where she splashed cold water on her cheeks. In the scrap of mirror nailed there she stared, bewitched, at two of the enormous women sliding over one another in an accomplished choreography of sweetness. They were as incredible to her as the creatures in an aquarium.

Robbie agreed to call her Lilac, too.

'Although it's not a colour I like,' he said. 'Why don't you go for something mysterious? Umber or cobalt or something tasty like peach?'

'Because it's Lilac, Lilac, Lilac,' she insisted, pushing him back on the mattress and bestriding him.

'All right. I surrender,' he gasped. 'Now there's a wee fellow down here wants to say hello to Lilac.'

Afterwards, sticky and replete, Lilac stretched back on the mattress. 'You'd miss the applause, wouldn't you?'

'Aye,' Robbie agreed. 'But it's nice to have a window.'

Evicted from his den under the college theatre, he had found a new squat at the top of a building marked for demolition in the Coombe. He rolled off the mattress and went to stand at the window.

'Don't shock the natives,' she scolded.

'If they could only see me through the rain,' he said. 'You know, I've a notion that the rain in Dublin is mostly Guinness.'

'Why's that?' She joined him at the window, her arm circling his straight waist.

'Well, if all the smoke that comes out of thon brewery condenses in the air, it must be spiking the rain.'

'Let's go out and taste it,' she laughed.

'Not me. I'm for the bed again.'

Lilac heaved the window open and leaned her head and shoulders out, turning her mouth up to drink from the teeming sky. When her hair was plastered wet she returned to the mattress.

'Now taste it.' She squeezed drops into his gaping mouth.

'Enough.' He shut his mouth and shook his head. 'You've disillusioned me. It tastes of shampoo and cinders.'

'I'm sorry.' Her hand smoothed his forehead. Pushing back his fringe, she found a scar tucked against his hairline. 'What's that?' She drew back, half-fearing that the slippery wound was still livid.

'My wee bit of history.' He laughed. 'Bogside, 1972.'

She soothed the scar with her lips, picturing the blood leaking down his face. 'You must have been only a child.'

'Oh, a little terrorist.'

Eleanor suspended her caresses to examine his face.

He grinned and cupped his hands around her chin. 'Not guilty, Your Honour.' He ran his finger over the mark. 'I forget it's there. My wee brother threw an ink bottle at me.'

'Seriously?'

'Cross my heart and hope to die,' he gabbled. 'And I poured blue blood.'

'Now I don't know what to believe.' She fell to kissing him again.

'Don't think about it,' he sighed under her.

To Frank she was already Red. But he wanted her to be more. He called for her one evening after work, his round face full with news. He laughed to find her sweeping the workshop. 'Don't tell me you're the gofer around here too.'

'Yep. Going backwards.' She leaned on a brush handle.

'You look like a monument. What would we call you? "The Working Woman" or "Cinderella"?'

'Don't be mocking me and get out of the way.'

'Come on.' He flung the brush from her hand and spun her around. 'I want to take you for a walk. I've something to tell you.'

'All right, all right, ' she panted as he set her down. 'But let me wash first.'

'Yes, water baby.' His finger streaked the dust coating her cheek.

By the time they crested Howth Head their own heads were giddy with climbing through gusty sea air. They flopped in the bracken and watched daylight stall in the endless dusk of summer.

'I like this time,' Frank said. 'As if everything is waiting.'

'The sky holding its breath.'

'Eleanor.' He canted onto his side and leaned over her. 'I got the job.'

'What?' She sat up. 'Oh Frank, that's great.' Her arm roped his neck and pulled him close. 'Well done,' she cheered. 'When do you start?'

'Next month.' He kissed her nose. 'You know what this means?' His tone grew serious.

'Yes.' She flashed a good-pupil smile. 'You're going to be an editor, top dog.'

'More than that.'

'More lolly?'

'I'm going to a new paper, Red. I won't be working for Dermot. So we can declare ourselves.'

'Yes.'

'And one day, Eleanor, I hope ... well ... will you marry me, Eleanor?'

'What?' Her arm dropped from his neck.

'Will you?'

She stared through him.

'You're not surprised, are you?'

'I don't know. I feel very young.'

'All the better,' Frank chivvied her. 'We'll have more time together.'

'I'm sorry, Frank.' She shut her eyes. 'I can't answer you now.'

'OK.' He tipped up her chin. 'Are you crying?'

'I think so.'

'Don't.' He kissed her eyes. 'I love you.'

'It's – overwhelming.' She tried to laugh and then blew her nose. 'Just give me time.'

Marriage. The word sounded foreign to her. For days she carried it around like an egg before presenting it to Louise.

'I agree with Frank,' her friend said. 'I don't know why you're surprised.'

'I never thought about it. That's all.'

'Does he know what he's letting himself in for?'

'What do you mean?'

'You can hardly even boil a kettle.'

'Neither can you.'

'I hope I never have to.'

Eleanor frowned. 'You will.'

'So, are you going to marry him?'

'I don't know.' Eleanor hesitated. 'I treasure him. He makes me feel warm and safe.'

'But?'

'I can't work it out. When he cares for me I feel like a child, but when he adores me I want to hurt him. To show that I don't need him. That I'm stronger than him.'

'You're screwed up.'

'No I'm not.'

'What about Robbie?'

'Robbie,' Eleanor relaxed into a smile. 'Robbie is Robbie. He's not serious. But yeah, I suppose I'd have to ditch him. Ditch a lot of things.'

'You don't have to marry him tomorrow.'

Gradually, Frank's proposal lulled Eleanor. Shrouded in cigarette smoke, she sat on her parents' headstone and absorbed the still air. It was the repose she shared with Frank, when they lay silent together for so long that she could feel through his skin, see through his eyes. Maybe dying together completed this union. No one knew who had died first, her mother or her father. They had fallen away from her life like a shell and left her shivering on the edge of a cliff. Now the thought of Frank filled her with a yearning for home. He would prevent her from falling off the cliff or flying. And the child that might rise from their love shook her with the violence of a limb wrenching free.

Most of all Eleanor wanted to talk to Katherine but her aunt was trekking in the Golden Triangle. She had taken to travelling lately, pressing ever farther from home to regions whose remoteness may have corresponded obscurely to unexamined areas of herself; the places which had been closed off by marriage.

'Cracked.' Dermot vented his incomprehension. 'Next stop Kabul, I suppose. She has responsibilities. She should have sown her wild oats before this.'

'The boys are able to look after themselves,' Angela pacified. 'Anyway, there's only Paul at home, now that Michael has gone to Galway.'

'Look at Tom.'

'What about him?'

'Well, I don't know what he's up to – do you? Here one day, gone the next. Teaching English. Sure there's no future in that.'

'He'll be back for our party.' Angela chuffed in the achievement of a twenty-five-year marriage.

'That's more than his mother will be, I suppose.'

'Ah well, I think it might be painful for Katherine,' Angela condoned.

'So you're only here for the nosh, too.' Tom nudged Eleanor when they lined up at the buffet table.

'And proud of it.' She laughed. 'I wanted to see you, in fact.'

Vanity sleeked Tom's tanned face. 'Well, let's get out of this mill,' he suggested, leading her across the garden to a rockery sown with pastel flowers.

'Sit here and be a gnome,' he said. 'I'm going to get us some alcohol.'

He returned with two glasses and a bottle of white wine which he set to cool in the tiny pond.

'Where's Rosemary?' He asked.

'Who?'

'Ronan.'

Eleanor laughed. 'I don't think he'd fancy that nickname.'

Tom slid her a testing look.

'He's in the States, on the trail of Frank Lloyd Wright. And working in a summer camp, minding rich kids who psych out on hash brownies.'

'While he tastes a few little buns.' Tom sniggered and refilled his glass.

'What about you?' She held out her own glass. 'Dermot says you're a waster.'

'Dermot's a prig.'

Eleanor pursed her lips. 'Not really. But he seems to think that he has to act like one.'

'Same difference.'

'Yeah, maybe.'

'You've got a boyfriend, I hear,' he teased.

'Big deal.' Eleanor flushed, catching in his glance the shared recollection of the lovers in the dunes.

'One lap to go.' Tom laughed softly in the memory. 'I'm glad, really. Will you introduce us?'

'Sometime, I suppose.'

'Has Mum met him?'

'Once. She was my alibi sometimes when I was meeting him secretly.'

'Are you going to marry him?'

'I might. What about you?'

'Well, all my little señoritas are in love with me,' Tom laughed.

'You're probably waiting for someone like your mother.'

'That sounds very Freudian.'

'Do you miss her?'

'Not when I'm away. But when I come home and she's gone, the house feels spooky. Like it's waiting. And I never know who'll be in my bed. There's always some waif or stray mooning around. The latest one is convinced my mother is a goddess.'

'What about you?'

'She's my ultimate hero, all right. Which doesn't mean that I go along with all her views – you know how adamant she is.' Tom shook his head. 'She has great legs.'

Eleanor chucked pebbles into the pond, building herself up to the next question. 'Did you ever fancy me?'

'That's a weird thing to ask.'

'Go on.'

'I don't know. Maybe when my balls were dropping I took a passing notion.'

'And now that they've dropped?'

He spread his arms ambivalently.

The sand was cooling under their bodies. Moonlight glittered on the fragments of bone and shell that coated their sweating skin.

'That was sweet,' Tom said.

'Sweet?' Eleanor leaned in on his chest to see his expression. His eyes were shut, his face curling with satisfaction.

'Sweet. Like the top note on a saxophone. You're a sweet little cousin.' His arm drew her into the notch of his neck.

'Not a real one, though,' she said, scooping and sifting the sand with her free hand. 'Do you remember, once, you talked about another place out there, like a mirror where we looked at ourselves?'

'Was I on acid?'

'No – at least I don't think so. It was that day – the couple and the radio. '

'Receiving signals from outer space?'

'You're only pretending not to remember.' She poured sand over his naked shoulder. 'I got there. I saw us. I stood up there and saw us together, here.'

'Sounds kinky.'

'It was only for a moment. But the moment went on and on. Like dream time. I want to live like that always, in one long moment. Seeing through life.'

'In other words you want to be God, and that

means you're mad.'

'I'm not.' She raised another fistful of sand and held it over his face. 'I'm going to bury us.'

The moon slipped over the sandy barrow and the sea retreated from the shore, like a parent closing the door on sleeping children.

'I know you remember,' Eleanor murmured.

Doubt tinged Dermot's face for weeks after Frank's proposal.

'Why can't you be glad for me?' Eleanor said.

'How is it that I always fall short of your measure?' Dermot despaired. 'I *am* glad, if you are confident that this is right for you. Just don't let yourself be rushed into it.'

'I thought you'd be pleased to get rid of me.'

'You're fishing now. You know that's not true.'

Angela was more acquiescent than her husband, but cautioned Eleanor. 'Dermot's right about biding your time. It's a big responsibility.'

'How old were you when you got married?'

'Twenty-three.'

'Do you ever regret it?'

'No.' Angela played with her rings. 'Not really. There were times when if divorce was available here I might have walked out the door.'

'Why?'

'I'm sure Dermot felt the same. You think of other

lives you could have lived. You resent the other person. But it wears off. Sometimes I used to take off my rings but an hour later I'd be rushing to put them on again.' She shivered and laughed at herself. 'I didn't have the confidence.'

Later, Eleanor listened in at their door.

'. . . it's understandable,' Angela was saying, 'she wants a family that is truly hers.'

'Not a second-hand one,' Dermot agreed wryly. 'I still say she's kidding herself: she's thrown this ball in the air to see what way it will fall. I even wonder how much she loves him.'

'You can't possibly assume these things.'

'Why not?' he sparked. 'I know her like a daughter. And I knew her father as if he was my brother.'

'But Eleanor is *not* her father.' Angela was impatient. 'That's the trouble, Dermot. You've spent all these years trying to make amends with Colm through his daughter.'

'Nonsense.'

'No, Dermot. You felt guilty because you didn't give him a job on the paper.'

'And have me smeared with the red brush, too? Anyway, he liked delivering letters. He said it gave him time to think.'

'And you chose to believe him. But now you think you were a coward.'

'I don't recall you inviting him to our "refined" dinner parties.'

'True. We both failed him . . .' Angela paused, '. . . them. But it's too late now for regrets. Let it go. Let Colm rest and let Eleanor be herself.'

Shame flared in the girl perched on the landing. She nursed the tender haven that Frank offered against a future of such humiliation. In the silence following this exchange, she identified Dermot's deeper conviction that he might have affected the course of her parents' lives.

'I can't let it go,' he said at last. 'I need a drink.'

The eavesdropper slid into the embrasure of Aoife's bedroom door but, too swift for her, Dermot reached in and seized her wrist.

'What's this behind the arras?' he hissed.

Eleanor emerged from the dark recess and allowed him to lead her down the stairs. He did not speak until he had a tumbler of whiskey in his hand.

'I suppose you enjoyed that little earful.'

'Not much.'

'Don't, for Christ's sake, tell me that you pity me.'

'I don't.'

He calmed under her direct look.

'You frighten me,' she continued, 'the way you give in to your gloom because you can't meet your own measure. We won't fritter our lives looking back over our shoulders.'

'We?' Dermot hitched his eyebrows. 'That's easier said than done. It's a middle-aged affliction.'

'Then we'll stay young,' she countered. 'Meanwhile, I think I should move out.'

'There's no need for that, Eleanor. This is your home.' His tone was subdued. 'Time for bed, I think.' He rose, and in passing, rested his hand on her shoulder.

Nevertheless, Eleanor did leave the house for a time.

She moved into Robbie's squat.

'So you want to play house?' He grinned when she turned up with her rucksack.

'If you'll let me.'

'As long as you're not wanting to play mummies and daddies that's cool.'

'No fear,' she laughed.

On the night when the exam results were posted up, Robbie towed home a band of his classmates, including Louise.

'Home sweet home, Nelly.' Louise winked. 'Very Boh-hip, with all those candles and oil lamps.'

'No electricity.'

'It must be freezing in winter.'

'There's a fireplace and we huddle up.'

'Why didn't you move in with Frank?'

Eleanor chilled. 'I didn't want to, and anyway, he wouldn't have approved.'

'Because of his mammy?'

'Partly. But also because of Dermot and Angela.'

'And he approves of this?' Louise belted out her laughter. 'I suppose it'll be a white wedding?'

'Don't be such a pain.'

'OK.' Louise peeved, then rummaged in her deep carpetbag saying, 'Here – Dad's started to import these from France.'

'Brilliant. Thanks.' Eleanor smiled at the indigo

box and the gypsy girl blithe in the clouds. She drew deeply on the high-tar tobacco, coasting its drift into foreignness. 'We have something a bit stronger here for tonight, as well,' she said.

'Goody, goody.' Louise rubbed her hands. 'I still can't believe I passed.'

'Neither can I.'

'Tough luck on Robbie.'

'Yes.' Eleanor wilted. 'Come on, let's have a smoke.'

'Not so fast, ladies.' Robbie draped his arms across the girls' necks as Eleanor began to skin a spliff. 'I've got a better idea.' His dipping accent sank to a drawl. 'George, here, forgot his bong. But I'm going to improvise.'

'How?' Eleanor laughed.

'Watch me.' He sidled to the windowsill and took down the teapot.

'The Mad Hatter's tea party!' George exclaimed.

' "The time has come," the Walrus said,' began a voice in the corner.

'Wait, wait.' A curly-headed girl jumped up. 'Everybody sit on the floor in a circle. That's it, nice and cosy: girl, boy; girl, boy; girl –'

'This is like a Paul Jones.'

'No,' George shouted. 'It's the Robbie Mac Pee tea ceremony.'

'What's that – a Molotov cocktail?'

'. . . "cabbages and kings" . . .'

'Something to put fire in your belly.'

'Well, I wish he'd hurry up,' Louise moaned. 'I'm going cold turkey already.'

'Coming, coming.' Robbie stepped towards the circle, bearing aloft the smouldering teapot.

'Hold it.' The curly-headed girl ordered silence. 'Everyone link hands and sing "Auld Lang Syne".'

'Piss off.'

'Yeah. Sit down and shut up.'

'No, folks, this is a lubricious occasion. We will not see his likes again.'

'Whose?'

'What's she talking about?'

'Lilac, put a sock in her mouth.'

'Do it yourself.'

'Peace. I bring heap big peace,' Robbie intoned, wedging himself between Eleanor and George. 'Now pass that around and let it all hang loose.'

'Amen.'

'It's like pass the parcel.' Eleanor grinned as the pot, travelling along the chain of hands, seemed to float and the faces dipped in its smoke rose bulging and pop-eyed, ready for the hit. Candlelight ambered the ring of foolish smiles and suddenly these were the only beings who mattered. Suffused with sensuous good will, she nuzzled Robbie.

'This is nice,' she said.

'Yes.' His arm tightened around her and his lips dabbed her forehead.

'I want it to last for ever.'

He smoothed her hair, then pulled away as the teapot approached. He inhaled and passed it over her head to George. Bending to her face, he opened her lips with his and shared the fumes with her. The dope slunk through her until it reached her head and transformed it into a wide echoing chamber. She smiled at Robbie, trying to pull him into her focus, like a watcher from another planet.

'Come in, Robbie, come in' – she was spiralling – 'there's room in my head for everyone.'

'I'm here,' he said, propping her. 'Are you OK?'

She frowned. 'You were disappearing.' Her eyes blinked slowly. 'There you are. You're back. I'm happy.' She curled against the boy.

Morning did not come for either of them and when Eleanor woke in mid-afternoon, the room squeezed in and out around her, as if the walls were on elastic. She closed her eyes and lay still. Robbie was snoring, a honk followed by a long whiffle. She had the impression that there were others in the room, and easing her head to the side, opened one eye only, fearing that the walls would bounce again if she opened both. She saw George stretched against the wall, her carton of Gitanes spilt open next to him. Shifting her head, she saw a girl and her partner rolled together in their coats. Eleanor closed her eyes, wishing they would all go away. It's Saturday, she thought. And we have no food. The munchies gaped in her stomach.

'Robbie, Robbie.' She pressed her mouth to his ear but the effort spun her head and she flopped back onto the mattress.

The next time she woke it was dark. Robbie was gone from her side. She sniffed a thick, spicy aroma.

'Robbie.'

He came and knelt by her side. 'Breakfast, dinner and tea served, Your Serendipitous Highness.' He smiled and ruffled her hair.

'What time is it?'

'Nine o'clock – PM.'

'We've lost a whole day.'

'Down the rabbit hole.' He laughed. 'Never to be seen again.' He took her hands and levered her to her feet.

She steadied and slowly familiarised herself with the room, like someone returned from a long voyage. 'You've cleaned up,' she observed.

'Aye, and The Pagoda cooked us dinner.'

The packing crate table was draped with one of her scarves, its pattern swarming in the flicker of three candles. Two cushions were drawn up at either side of the table.

'My cigarettes,' she said vaguely.

Robbie pointed to the bookshelf where the moon-lit gypsy brandished her tambourine.

'Did you try one?'

He shook his head. 'I was waiting for you to offer me one.'

'What's mine is yours.' She gestured expansively.

'Is it, Mrs Mulvey?'

'Fuck Louise.'

Robbie wagged his finger. 'It wasn't Louise.'

She moved warily to the bookshelf and drew two cigarettes from the blue box, lit both, and handed one to Robbie. 'Who then?'

'Your brother.'

'Ronan?'

Robbie nodded. 'Wait up' – he stalled her outburst – 'before you go poking his eyes out.'

The strong smoke poured furiously from her mouth and nostrils.

'He came here looking for you. There's some trouble at home.'

'How did he –?'

'Louise, I suppose.' He plucked a shred of tobacco off his tongue. 'Anyway, he was a bit confused to see me and blurted something about Frank, so I wheedled the story out of him. The Special Branch would have been proud of me.'

Eleanor laughed. 'You don't seem too put out.'

'We're not handcuffed together,' he said. 'I *was* a wee bit surprised. Is Frank the fat lad you told me about?'

She nodded.

'I didn't think you were keen for the high jump.'

'Neither did I.'

When they had pinched the last grains of rice off their plates Eleanor asked the question which had lain coiled in her mind since the previous evening.

'What are you going to do now?'

He toyed with his knife before looking up to answer. 'I'm taking off.'

'Off? Where to?'

'Going to busk my way around the world.'

'Don't you want to be a doctor?'

'Who wants to spend their life with sick people?'

'Then why did you choose medicine in the first place?'

'I had to do something. It sounded impressive. Saving lives and all that. But I got sick of learning about the mighty mitochondrion and I realised that I actually don't care. All this Sunday school stuff doesn't hold piss in the real world.'

'It doesn't say that everyone has to be a doctor.'

'No, and it doesn't tell you that people look out for theirselves and no one gives a damn about you or me.'

'I do.'

He sighed. 'What about Fatty Frank?'

'Don't call him that. You're the one who said we weren't tied together.'

'That's the point. We were in it for what we could get.'

'But it was nice.'

'Yes, Lilac. Or Eleanor. Or whoever you are. It was nice.'

'I'll miss you and wee Johnny.' Eleanor's face wavered.

'Name the first one after me.'

'Sure.'

Sayonara, she thought, sayonara to all the ones who had flashed in and out of her life leaving their imprint in her heart.

The trouble at home brooded in Dermot's and Angela's faces. It was Angela who told Eleanor that Katherine was dying.

'No,' she refused. 'It's not true.'

'I'm afraid so,' Angela said. 'Remember she was sick when she came home?'

'But that was only Bangkok belly.'

'That's what we all thought at the time.'

'Can't she get treatment? Radium or something?'

Angela sighed. 'She doesn't want it. She says it'll only prolong the pain, not cure it.'

'It's not fair.' Eleanor's head bowed, the nearness of that loss displacing her. 'Katherine is too good to die.' Air and light went away, but Katherine's breezy laugh and angular grace rose vividly in her. She refused to see their eclipse. 'She won't die. She won't die.' Eleanor flailed, her voice aching urgency.

'She wants to see you,' Angela said after a few moments.

'I'll tell her,' she said, 'I'll tell her she can't die.'

Fiercely, already, she felt her arms clasp the woman's lean body against death and infuse it with her own bright life.

To Eleanor's relief her long ring on the presbytery bell was answered by Ray.

'Eleanor?' He peered into the dark before swinging back the door. 'What are you doing here at this hour?'

'I've been walking. Walking all night.' She shivered. 'I didn't feel like going home.'

He settled her beside a fake coal fire in the parlour and brought in a tea tray. 'I take it you haven't eaten.'

'I didn't think I was hungry.'

'So what's the problem?' Ray lit a cigarette and watched his niece tear nervously at her food.

'It's Katherine,' she gulped. 'Oh, Ray. It's terrible.'

The mantelpiece clock chimed eleven.

'She's going to die and I can't – I can't –' Her look beseeched him. 'I don't know what to do.'

'There is nothing you can do.' He spoke gently. 'Except – are you sure?'

She shut her eyes and nodded.

'Have you seen her?'

'That's just it, Ray. You wouldn't believe her. She talks about it as if . . . well . . . in a matter-of-fact way. She wants me to make her grave – that's how serene she is.'

'I can believe it. But maybe, too, she's being brave for your sake.'

'No. She is looking straight at death.' Eleanor frowned with conviction, then broke into a wry grin.

'You know, I used to think that I could do that. I thought, I've been there, I know death. But still it intimidates me and makes me angry.'

' "Do not go gentle" . . .'

'It seems so lonely.'

'Does Katherine have the faith?'

'Oooh. Don't come the priesteen.'

'Eleanor. Why can't you accept that I *am* a priest?'

'I'm sorry.' She offered him a cigarette. 'In fact, she's taken to Buddhism.'

Ray winced.

'What's wrong with that?'

'Nothing' – he fumbled in his match box – 'except that I'm tired of trendy Eastern mysticism. I mean, what has Buddha got that Christ doesn't have?'

'Katherine likes the tranquillity of Buddhism and the way it sees all of life flowing in one great stream.'

'Does she really believe in reincarnation?'

'She's not sure. She says she doesn't want to come back as a monkey. Her biggest regret is not getting to an ashram.'

'She can do that in her next life.'

'Not if she's a monkey,' Eleanor laughed.

'What does she want on her tombstone?'

'It's not exactly a tomb. She wants to be cremated but she wants her ashes spread in a mini Zen garden.'

'What's that when it's at home?'

'Well, it's at home in a monastery. It's made with raked gravel and rocks representing the sea or rivers and mountains. The patterns are guided by meditation. Then people come and meditate on them. Katherine lent me books about it.'

'I hope you're not about to go traipsing to Shangri-la.'

'Don't be a stick in the mud, Ray.'

'All right,' Ray said. 'Now, let me give you a lift home.'

Eleanor seized his arm. 'Can I sleep here tonight, Ray?' Her grip pressed him.

'We've no spare rooms at the moment.'

'I can sleep on the floor of your room.'

He laughed. 'That might compromise me.'

'But I'm your *niece*.'

'I think my superiors might say, "pull the other one".'

'Well, I'll sleep here on the sofa.'

'And give Mrs Hegarty a heart attack in the morning? No. Better in my room. I'll kip here.' He opened a cupboard in the corner of the room, and lifting out a bottle of whiskey, poured a finger each into two tumblers. 'You need more than tea and electricity to warm you in this place.'

By the time they reached Ray's bedroom she was light with the effect of grief and alcohol. Eleanor watched him move about the room, which was bare of personal trivia. Within him she sensed an unreachable starkness, reluctantly covered by the street man.

'Will you be all right here?'

'Fine.' She sat on the bed and patted it. 'Hey, thanks, Ray.'

'You're welcome.' He smiled.

She had never slept in such a quiet place. The silence was annihilation. It was a thing which clambered over her and slicked her skin and saturated her with the feverish dreams of blank men. Once, in its depth, when she flinched alert, she saw the moon-barred window and tried to pitch a cry, but her voice was stifled by the silence.

Frank and Eleanor allowed the darkness to absorb them until the city winked into view. Overhead the parallel curve of sodium lamps tracked their course to infinity.

She rested her head against the back of the seat. 'I can't do it, Frank.'

His eyes cut from the rear-view mirror to the wing mirror. His left hand went from his knee to the gear shift and back. The car swung into the fast lane. 'I know.'

'Don't think ... I mean, it's nothing to do with your mother. She was great – and all that food! It's me. I don't –'

'I said, I know.'

'Then why?'

He shook his head. 'I love you, Eleanor. I had to try. Or I'd have regretted it all my life.'

Her throat hardened. The lights on the road dissolved. 'I love you, Frank, but I couldn't live – I couldn't be –'

'Stop it, Eleanor. Stop it.' His hands clenched the wheel.

Desolate motor showrooms flagged by.

She snivelled, tried a laugh. 'I feel so stupid.'

'Don't say any more.'

Her relief seemed to dance on his thwarted eagerness. Being loved confers fateful power. She had deformed this man's future. Remorse nagged her almost to unsay the words. This day out had been the first step into the life they would make for themselves. Frank, elated at taking off in his brother-in-law's big car, had spun a jokey spiel, marking sights along the route: the Curragh, where sheep ignored the traffic and an occasional horse thundered on the green plain; the Aga Khan's pink cottage; Moore Abbey, whose walls ring with the Count's pure tenor; and then the prison, islanded by barbed wire and sentries. Frank's gesturing hand had dropped to take hers, fear for the vulnerability of their happiness travelling between them.

'I think we should change the name of the town,' he had said.

'Because everyone thinks of Portlaoise as a prison?'

'Yes.'

'You wanted to escape.'

'True. But I've mellowed. It looks better today, with you.'

His lips had touched hers, and she had broken away, suddenly needing air.

Now, all the signposts on their road were annulled by her ingratitude. When the car drew up outside the house Eleanor hesitated, then, beneath the fold of her shawl, worried the ring off her spastic hand.

'Are you –? Will you –?'

'Please go, Eleanor.' Frank's shoulders convulsed. His forehead dropped to the steering wheel. 'Leave me be,' he whispered.

She shut the door, extinguishing the glister of the solitaire on the black leather seat.

The next day Dermot reserved his 'I told you sos', but his face was smug.

Angela was disbelieving, then turned sorrowful on Frank's account. 'He must be desperately hurt,' she said.

'Don't rub it in,' Eleanor implored.

Angela sighed. 'You know best, I suppose.'

Eleanor laughed and threw her arm around Angela's neck. 'That's the first time you've ever said that.'

Angela rallied. 'Well, at least we hadn't started on the wedding plans.'

'Wise woman,' Dermot interjected. 'Practical to the last.'

Aoife was the one who most regretted the split. She came to Eleanor's room that night and was surprised to find the older girl's face swept with tears.

'Why are you crying?'

'I don't know,' Eleanor said. 'I don't know.'

Aoife climbed onto the bed. 'Do you still love Frank?'

'It's not that.' Eleanor pouted. 'It's as if a wall has collapsed but I can't see past the rubble.'

'You could go back to him.'

'Never.'

'I wish you would.' Aoife's head tilted in a plea.

'I'm sorry.' Eleanor smiled ruefully. 'I've spoilt your chance to be a bridesmaid.'

'I wanted to be an auntie.'

'Well, life won't end because I'm not marrying Frank.'

Eleanor's life somersaulted when Louise announced her coming-of-age surprise for Ronan. To start his birthday celebrations, his sisters served him breakfast in bed.

He groped instinctively for his glasses on the bedside locker. 'Thanks, girls.' He plumped himself up against the pillows. 'This is it, the big day. The key of the door. The young hero steps into the world with his sausages in his gob.' He cackled and tucked into the fry. 'I feel different already.'

'Indigestion,' Eleanor quipped. 'Back to cornflakes tomorrow.'

'Aoife will bring me breakfast, won't you?'

'No way. You can bring ours. We've been slaving all week.'

'I hope Mamma's in the kitchen baking apple pie.'

'Everything is made already,' Eleanor assured him. 'All we have to do is scoff it.'

'Yes,' Aoife chimed, 'and you have to blow out all your candles in one go.'

'Phew !' The birthday boy gasped elaborately. 'I'm glad I'm not eighty-one today.'

The party was to be what Dermot described as 'an Angela promotion'. The house brimmed with balloons and streamers and swelled at the back into a red and white striped marquee. Coloured oil wheeled plasmically around the tented ceiling while Felix the Cat and the Sorcerer's Apprentice skittered across the canvas walls.

Louise drew Eleanor aside and told her under cover of the pogo beat that she was expecting Ronan's child.

'Funny ha ha,' Eleanor said.

'Ronan didn't believe me either.'

'You didn't say it to him?'

'Of course I did.' Louise was affronted. 'He has a right to know.'

'It's not a very funny joke.'

'I wish it was a joke.'

Eleanor scanned Louise's lovely eyes and shut her own against what she saw there.

'Are you going to keep it?'

'I'm going to have it, if that's what you mean. After that, I don't know,' Louise said.

'But – *Ronan*?' Eleanor, offended at her exclusion, strained to understand.

'It was nothing serious. We slept together now and again. No strings.'

'Just an umbilical cord.'

'We didn't plan that.'

'How come neither of you told me?'

'That would have complicated things.'

Eleanor pulled ferociously on her cigarette. 'I see, but now that it is complicated it's OK to tell me?'

'Yes.'

'How long has Ronan known about the baby?'

Louise consulted her watch. 'Almost half an hour.'

'You are unbelievable!' Eleanor rounded on her friend.

'Birthday present.'

'I'm going to see if he's all right.'

'Leave him for the moment.' Louise held her back. 'Look, he's in a group. Dance with me, Nelly.'

Veered by Louise's teasing mew, Eleanor crushed her cigarette and grinned. 'A baby. I don't believe it.' She hooked her friend's arm and together they pressed into the bop.

The grin returned when Eleanor woke the next day. Surfacing out of her hungover blur, the thought of Louise and Ronan's baby rose fresh and beamed before her.

'Didn't you see the "DO NOT DISTURB" sign?' Ronan rasped when he saw her standing by his bed. 'Go away. I want to be left to die in peace.' He rolled over.

'Rise and shine, Daddy.' Eleanor swung the curtains open.

'Shut up.' Ronan flung his arm over his eyes to block the light.

'Don't panic. They're at mass, where you should be.'

'I'm glad you think it's so funny.'

'Are you going to marry her?'

'What do you think? I only just got the key of the fucking door. I'm not about to lock myself in.'

'That's all right.'

'Good. Now please fuck off.'

Louise was more gracious than Ronan.

Eleanor woke her friend with a cup of tea. 'Dermot used to bring Angela a cuppa every morning when she was expecting Aoife. She said she couldn't get out of bed without it.'

'Thanks, doc.' Louise dragged herself up. 'The worst is nearly over, I hope.'

'How far are you gone?'

'Just three months.'

'What are you going to do?'

'Go away.'

'Do your parents know?'

Louise shook her head. 'I'll drop out for the rest of the year and tell them I want to travel for a few months.'

'Have you any money?'

'A little – I don't suppose you have any to spare?'

'No.'

'Well, it's been nice knowing you.' She curled into the wall.

'I'm coming with you.'

'What?'

'I'm coming with you.'

'Wheeee!' Louise leapt up and seized Eleanor's waist. 'That's my Nelly-nor,' she cheered, then staggered. 'Oops. Maybe Angie was right about the tea.' She eased herself onto the bed. 'We'll elope – what an adventure.'

'Yes.' Eleanor bobbed on the generous surprise of relief.

'What'll you tell your folks?'

'Same thing. That I'm going away to get over Frank. I have the money I started to save with him.'

'How do I even know it's mine?' Ronan asked that evening.

'It is.' Eleanor said.

'What makes you so positive?' He halted to challenge her.

The shadows of the half-lit street intensified the marks of anxiety on his face. On the pretext of 'clearing their heads', they had stepped out of the house to talk openly.

'Louise doesn't have any other lovers at the moment.'

'Well, to hear her talk you'd swear she was fighting them off.'

'Robbie said she's not popular in college.'

'She's done this deliberately, then.' Ronan hawked and spat. 'As an excuse to get out.'

'Don't be stupid. Anyway, she'll probably go back after she's had the baby.'

'We'll see,' he snorted. 'I don't understand why she's insisting on having it.'

'It's not like squashing flies, you know.'

'Well, well. And I thought you were liberated.'

'I am,' she said, 'but it's not easy one way or the other.'

'I'd help her if she wanted to get rid of it.'

'Not if she has it?'

'No. I don't want it and I've given her the option not to have it.'

Eleanor's spirit dimmed. 'I never thought you were such a shit, Ronan.'

'All men are monsters,' he taunted. 'Isn't that what the sisterhood says?'

'I wasn't listening.' Eleanor turned from him and retraced her steps to the house.

Bill's face soured when Eleanor said she was leaving. 'What about all those little angels you were touching up?' He angered. 'Hey? You can't just walk out in the middle of a job.'

She recoiled from the waft of menace.

'Hey? Hey?' His voice encroached. 'You're a little snob, that's what you are.'

She looked into the face ugly with resentment.

'Fuck your angels,' she said. 'You've screwed enough blood out of me.'

He quivered, then broke in a flat, dark laugh. 'Ha, Lilac. I should have known better than to tangle with a redhead.'

'My name's not Lilac. It's Eleanor.'

His face twitched. 'So who's on your tail, girlie?'

'No one. Just give me my wages.'

'OK, OK.' He thumbed a wad of notes from his pocket. 'Yeah, maybe it's for the best. I don't know what kind of trouble you're in, but I don't need it.'

Jarlath pressed a rag to mock tears when Eleanor

said goodbye. 'You can take His Holiness with you.'

'Keep him in memory of me.'

She entrusted her plans for Katherine's memorial to him.

The boy was vexed by her departure. 'Now I'm stuck with the quare fella.'

'Sorry, Jarlath.' She smiled. 'Put a muzzle on him.'

She had three more farewells to make.

'Silly, isn't it?' Eleanor was peeling a scab of lichen off her parents' headstone. 'There's nothing in there only old bones.'

'That's not the point,' Ray said. 'It's a place to remember them, to pay your respects. Their souls are preparing the way for you.'

'No, I don't want them leaning over me any more.' Her shoulders hunched quickly. 'Colm Leyden and his beloved wife Margaret,' she read aloud. 'I know that stone better than I knew them. Why is there no epitaph?'

'No one could think of one, I suppose. Colm wouldn't have been too keen on a prayer. He had to suffer the funeral.' Ray grinned apologetically.

'What about that thing you said once about "not going gently"?'

'"Do not go gentle into that good night". It's a poem. "Rage, rage against the dying of the light".'

'They didn't get a chance to rage. Their light was switched off.'

'Who knows what passed through their minds in those last minutes.'

'I used to think I did. And that I belonged there, in a

way. The stone was like an anchor.' Eleanor stood back. 'Not any more. I'll never visit it again. Good-bye,' she said softly and started down the path.

Ray caught up with her outside the gate. 'Are you all right?'

'Yes.' Her eyes smarted. 'Put that on the stone, will you, Ray? "Rage against the dying of the light".'

'If you like.'

'It's good advice.'

'At least you had the stone, Eleanor,' he said solemnly. 'And the names.'

'What do you mean?'

'I'm thinking of the child. Who will be its parents?'

'Louise may not give it away.'

'You talk as it if was an unwanted gift, being passed from hand to hand.'

'Everybody makes mistakes, Ray. *You* should give her credit for having it.'

'I do, I do.' The priest's face was tired. 'I dislike the flippancy. "A mistake", you call it, but it's another human life. Not theirs to play around with.'

'I shouldn't have told you.' She looked away from him.

'No, you were right.' He tried to lighten his voice. 'Someone has to know what the pair of you are up to.'

'I'll send you an address as soon as I can,' she said, her eyes still set on the sea.

'You're doing a good thing, Eleanor. And I love you.' His hand brushed her shoulder. 'I'll fix up the stone.'

'Thanks, Ray.' The curve of the bay unsteadied.

Eleanor put her hand to the warm trace of Ray's touch. 'I will rage,' she said, hearing his bike rev into the slipstream of passing traffic.

Katherine and Eleanor abbreviated their goodbyes.

'I won't be here, when – or if – you come back.'

Or if. Eleanor stayed the elation of the journey already begun in her. 'Don't say that.' She gestured impatiently.

'All right. We won't be morbid. But tell me what you are running away from.'

'Nothing,' Eleanor sparked.

Katherine shook her wasted head. 'I know, I know.'

Eleanor turned away from her aunt's look.

'That's the thing about partings. They make you cut through the bullshit.'

Their talk hushed under the onset of the winter evening.

Katherine sank against her cushion. 'You must go now,' she said faintly, her teeth plucking her lips against the lash of pain.

'Is there anything I can do?' Eleanor moved to her side.

Katherine's head thrashed convulsively for a few moments, then her hand lifted. Eleanor kissed it, her lips grazing the fine bones beneath the veil of skin.

Tom saw her out.

'I'm sorry.' She touched his arm.

'We'll be all right.' He braced himself.

'Oh God. What time is it? Where are we?'
Louise's head slumped against Eleanor's
shoulder.

'Between nowhere and nowhere.' Eleanor could
pry no crack in the darkness. Her heart quickened to
the speed of the train driving them towards the
surprise of light.

'I feel awful, Nelly.'

'I know, but try and rest,' Eleanor soothed. 'Your
man's smelly socks are giving me the collywobbles,
too.' She wrinkled her nose.

'No little wifey to wash them.' Louise yawned and
resettled against her friend.

The chateau dominated the town. Its walls, crowned
by the sun, complicated the streets with shade.

'This is it.' Eleanor savoured the lustre of foreignness. 'The start of the adventure.'

'Can we postpone it until I've had a rest?' Louise
crouched on her rucksack.

'OK. You and the bags wait on a bench and I'll look for a pension.'

'*Pens-i-on*,' Louise stressed. 'Make them write down the price.'

Eleanor returned, smiling, and prodded her drowsing friend. 'I've found one. It's called Les Bleuets and Madame's name is Mireille. I think we're the first visitors this year.'

'Carry me, Nelly,' Louise moaned.

'Get lost. It's not far.' She helped her up and curved her arm around Louise's waist.

Mireille hailed Eleanor as an old friend already, and batting her wheezing chest, dispatched a young girl to trudge the guests up the three flights of stairs to their room.

Louise sagged onto the bed, and rolling over, sighed asleep. A table and two chairs waited at the centre of the room. Eleanor sat, instilling the grain of the place that would shelter them for over a year.

Louise headed the job hunt. Through the window of the Café Aurore, Eleanor watched her fling last-ditch smiles at the proprietor.

'You should have stayed with me,' Louise snapped when she rejoined her.

'I'm sick of begging.'

'Well, I'm the one doing the talking. The good news is he's agreed to take us. You in the kitchen, me on the floor.'

Eleanor waited for the catch.

'He's not paying you very much – but I'll get tips.'

'I knew it.' Eleanor glowered through the plate

glass. 'They're all the bleeding same.'

Louise shut her eyes. 'Yes, yes,' she placated, 'but we don't have a choice.'

'They pretend they're doing me a favour. After all, I'm only half a person,' Eleanor jibed. 'Wait till they discover you're two people.'

'That's just it, I have to take this job. You can come along if you want to. We'll pool the money.'

'I don't *want* to.'

'Up to you.' Louise wearied. 'You said it yourself. They're all the same.'

Eleanor suppressed the sob of impotence. Some day, some day, the chant of justice tapped in her. 'All right,' she yielded. 'For the baby.'

'Thanks, pal.' Louise linked her friend's arm. 'I'll stand you an espresso.'

In the kitchen Eleanor took orders from the chef and made faces behind his back with Alexandre, the commis, who helped her on the sly to do the spirit-breaking tasks set by the chef. She did not need to understand the man's words to know when he was railing at her.

'*Patates! Patates!*' He hit at her weak vocabulary one day. '*Les patates sont pour les cochons!*'

She shrugged blankly.

'Pick, pick,' Alexandre said and snorted, '*pick.*'

'Oh – *pig.*' Eleanor smiled.

'*Oui. Patates* for pick. Not for man.'

'Then what – *qu'est-que c'est?*' She held up a potato.

'*Pomme de terre,*' he translated. '*Pommes de terre: pommes frites; pommes sautées; pommes dauphinoise;*

pommes duchesse; pompon.' He swung around, poising the potato on his wiggling butt.

Eleanor burst into laughter.

'*Salaud,*' the chef growled and thwacked Alexandre's ear with a cloth.

Eleanor dodged into the scullery where an old man pored eternally over a sinkful of greasy pots and delf.

'Can I help?' She gestured to him.

'*Non, non.*' Mahmet retreated, eyes darting towards the kitchen.

'OK. *D'accord.*' Eleanor moved away, recognising the frustration in the man's terror.

Here, Eleanor was frequently alone. Her time off did not always coincide with her friend's and as Louise's pregnancy advanced, she wanted only to sleep when she was released from the café. Eleanor, bristling with a hungry energy, climbed the town's narrow streets to the castle, where she passed through the moribund rooms to emerge on the ramparts. Her body pressed to the sandstone ledge, she faced into the spring breeze, wanting the unfamiliar air to lift her. She felt like one of Ray's birds, cruising in the exhilaration of departure.

'Now I know why that creep took us on.' Louise slammed onto the bed and kicked her shoes high into the air.

'Watch it.' Eleanor ducked.

'He tried to feel me up. Right there, behind the counter, as if I was a cat.'

'What did you do?'

'I ground my heel into his toe and didn't go behind the counter for the rest of the day.' She convulsed with sudden laughter. 'He was hopping.'

'Does he know you're pregnant?'

Louise sniggered. 'I suppose so, but he's not letting on.'

'Are you going to quit?'

'Are you mad?'

'But he'll try again.' Eleanor was aghast. 'Besides, it's an insult.'

'I can't afford to stand on a principle.' Louise lay back, resigned. 'I can handle him.'

Instead, it was Eleanor who left the Café Aurore. Halfway through slopping out the kitchen floor some weeks later, she paused, attending the afternoon lull. Through the scullery door she glimpsed Mahmet dozing on an upturned crate. From the bar came the to and fro of the chef and *patron* arguing about *le foot*. '*Allez les Verts*,' bellowed the chef. A fly sizzled on the ultra-violet strip. How many more times must she mop this floor? She looked from the scummy water to the tide mark that showed how far she had come. The clean area dried imperceptibly into the uncleaned part. Her life was stopped by a broken red floor. Standing the mop in the bucket, she untied her apron and said to the dying flies, 'Let him mop his own fucking mess.' For good measure she spat onto the wet tiles. Outside, she lit a cigarette, waiting for the happy surge of smoke in her lungs.

At the end of Eleanor's first week in her new job the girls celebrated on a big tip earned by Louise.

'What did you do to get this?' Eleanor teased.

'Natural charm,' Louise simpered. 'At least, he was charmed, but she was giving me funny looks.'

'Home-wrecker.'

'Yeah.' The tapered eyes looked wistful. 'I could have thrown a leg over him.'

Eleanor laughed. 'Here's to other people's husbands.'

Their glasses rang together.

'So how are things *chez* Mme Riche?'

'Fine.' Eleanor was smug. 'When I finish ironing her camisoles I sit around eating chocolates and reading *Marie Claire*.'

'You bitch. I should have that job.'

'You wouldn't meet any hunks.'

'What about M. Riche?'

'There seems to be more than one M. Riche.'

'Ah ha! That explains the bonbons.' Louise winked.

'*Oui, oui*. But she says she has to mind her figure,' Eleanor said. 'She's on a *régime*.'

'The double bind,' Louise bemoaned. 'Women slim to attract men and men woo them with sweets and fancy dinners.'

'Speak for yourself,' Eleanor retorted. 'Some men like fat women.'

'You better keep scoffing the chocolates, so,' Louise laughed.

Eleanor was fascinated by the growth of Louise's body. The baby seemed to be filling it drop by drop, like a rain barrel. Louise's flesh, softly buffed by the temperate sun, had amplified to cocoon her and the child in a tranquil abeyance. That quiet possessed its own power of stored sensuality and Eleanor could not get enough of looking at her, until one night her hand reached for the charged limbs. With a soft cluck Louise inclined to the bemused caress. Eleanor flushed against her bringing her lips to the sweat-filmed shoulder while her hand smooched into Louise's vulva, delight springing in her own. Louise's legs scissored shut.

'What the fuck are you doing?' She seethed, suddenly alert.

'Just that.' Eleanor drew her hand away and sucked her finger, grinning at the petulant flash of Louise's eyes. 'What's wrong?'

'If it's not the *patron*, it's you. Will no one leave my body alone?' Louise heaved against the wall.

'But we're friends.' Eleanor ran her finger down her friend's spine. 'I'll let you play with my pussy if you let me play with yours.'

Her friend flinched. 'Get lost.'

'So you are a prude,' Eleanor murmured and rolled away, shaking in the loneliness of a letdown.

'Don't ever try that again,' Louise said the next evening.

'Big deal.' Eleanor tried to deflect her friend.

'You're either perverted or desperate.'

'I'll never touch you again.' Eleanor raised her hand in oath.

'Apart from anything else, you seem to forget that I'm pregnant.' Louise drove cigarette smoke down her nostrils. 'Or maybe you don't care.'

'I came with you, didn't I?'

'You were dying to get away.' The dark eyes fixed on Eleanor. 'You came because it makes you feel morally superior.'

'I came for you and for the baby.'

'It's no fun being pregnant, you know.' Louise hit her stride. 'But of course you don't. Your little friends probably couldn't even get it up.' Her laugh was arid.

'You bitch.' Eleanor stormed from the room.

The night streets were quiet, low gusts of café voices scoring their emptiness. From an alleyway came the sound of a man urinating. She circled the town until, finding the bench she and Louise had rested on the day they arrived, she sat and lit a cigarette. Above her the castle walls blocked out the sky. As she stared they shifted, inching closer, poised like the crest of a wave to tumble over her. Her breath shortened, then stopped. She flung away the cigarette and twisted her head, straining for air. She was suffocating. Panic flapped in her chest. She tried to stand and flee the encroaching wall but her legs cracked and she stumbled. She dragged herself across the square and fell thrashing in a feverish sweat on the edge of the path.

The standoff between the friends lasted for four days. Eleanor unrolled her sleeping bag and slept on the floor, and Louise stepped over her to get in and out of bed. Then, with her beguiling capacity to change the weather, Louise greeted Eleanor one evening with a bottle of sparkling wine.

'What kept you?' she chirped, filling two glasses. 'This had almost boiled.'

Eleanor flopped into her chair. 'Mme Riche was like a cat that's lost her kittens today.'

'Well, drink this to cheer you up – from the *patron*, for the *bébé*.' Louise raised her glass. 'He says he'll keep the job for me.'

'I have something, too.' Eleanor grinned and pulled a heart-shaped box of chocolates from her bag. 'Mme Riche slipped me these when I was leaving.'

'She wants to fatten you up.'

Eleanor shook her head. 'M. Riche is home.'

'Ooh.' Louise ogled for the gossip. 'So? What's he like?'

'Hard to say. He only surfaced at about three o'clock and then drifted around in a kimono, muttering about his *nuit blanche*.'

'Didn't he say anything to you?'

'No, but I heard him asking her about the *bonne*. He

mustn't have been too happy because she said I was *très raisonnable*. Then she said, *Irlandaise*, and he burst out – *Le Taxi mauve*. He said it about three times. After that he kept grinning at me, as if I had slid in off a rainbow.'

'Nelly the leprechaun,' Louise heralded. 'And the chocs are to buy your silence, I suppose.'

'Or to bury the evidence.'

'Poor M. Riche.'

'Poor eejit.'

'Oh well, eat drink and be merry, for soon we'll be mammies!'

'Here's to the *patron*.'

'Here's to M. Riche.'

'Here's to *bébé*.'

'I wonder if it's a boy or a girl.'

Bébé was a boy. Joy astonished Eleanor when he warmed the ingle of her arm.

'I can't believe how beautiful he is.' She beamed at Louise.

Refulgent, Louise agreed and reached out her plump arms to take him again. 'Does he look like me?' she murmured into the serious red face.

'With a pair of specs on he might look like Ronan.' Eleanor laughed.

'I'm sure he'll take after me,' Louise said coldly.

'That'll be tough.' Eleanor's finger stroked the infant hair.

The babe inspired open-handed tenderness everywhere. Mireille had a cradle installed in the girls' room. Flowers and sugared almonds came from her neighbours, and Mme Riche presented a box bubbling with ribbons.

'She looked a bit sad when she gave it to me,' Eleanor said.

'No *petits* Riches?' The new mother expanded with

sympathy.

Eleanor shook her head.

'He'll be a right sea dog in this !' Louise marvelled at the miniature sailor suit. 'We'll have to buy him a toy boat.'

Abruptly, and with head averted, Eleanor said, 'You're not giving him away, are you, Louise?'

'I don't think so.' She sighed heavily. 'But Nelly, how will we keep him?'

Gladness buoyed Eleanor. 'We'll manage' – she took Louise's hand – 'we'll manage some way.'

'You win. Or he does.'

'We have to give him a name.'

'He has one,' Louise announced: 'Homer.'

'Homer? Not really?'

'I'm serious. Like the blind poet who wrote about the Greek heroes. Stavvy was a big fan.'

'Oh.' Eleanor looked with pity at the pocket-sized creature in front of her. 'Isn't that a bit of a millstone?'

'He doesn't have to write poetry. I like the name,' Louise said. 'You didn't expect me to call him Ronan, did you?'

'No. I think that calling a child after someone is like wanting the child to resemble that person.'

'I hope not.' Horror rolled in Louise's eyes. 'I was named after one of mother's mutton-dressed-as-lamb friends. What about you?'

'My granny. She said names are like jam labels.'

'Sweet,' Louise simpered. 'I thought it was Eleanor Marx – not that I'm expecting you to throw yourself under a bus.'

'Sister Noonan told me there was a French queen

called Aliénor, but she became a nun.' Her namesake grimaced.

'And there's Eleanor Rigby, and Little Nell,' Louise mused. 'You're a lonely lot, you Eleanors.'

Even as she doted to folly on Louise's child, Eleanor was shadowed with loneliness. The baby fledged a bright peace in her, sensitising all her thoughts. Throughout the day she craved his presence in the ghosted space where once she had felt her own maybe child, and paused now and then, imagining she heard his yell. Her love knew every speck of the body whose tininess was emphasised by dusky folds of skin at his joints. Already the eyes had their mother's lanceolate shape but the brief dark eyebrows were taut with surprise.

'It's the purest form of love,' Louise declared once, pillowing the child against her exorbitant bosom. 'He thinks the world of me.'

'Does he think at all?' Eleanor needled.

'Of course he does. He's very wise.' His mother kissed his forehead.

Motherhood absorbed Louise, withdrawing her into possessiveness and a mystique of hidden knowledge, the undreamt pangs and discomforts brought on by the baby and confided to Mireille were beyond explaining to her childless friend. When Eleanor lulled the infant to sleep she was aware of the tapered eyes sliding strangely over her. She caught those eyes, too, off guard, contemplating her crooked arm, until she wanted to scream, 'It's not the plague.' They both laughed when the pinkie penis champagned piss in their faces, but Louise took special delight if Eleanor was the target.

'That's what he thinks of you, Nelly,' she would cackle and deftly enfold the small bum in its envelope. 'He's a smart arse.'

'And you're becoming a pain in the arse,' Eleanor let go at last.

'What do you mean?'

'I'm just the breadwinner around here. You hardly let me near the baby, as if – as if you think I'm trying to steal him.'

'You're paranoid.'

'I'm not. But I love him and I want to share him,' Eleanor pleaded. 'After all, I am his auntie.'

'There's not a drop of your blood in him.'

'Then I'm his surrogate father.'

'Do you want to give the child a complex?'

'Joke. Joke.' Eleanor gave up.

Louise brooked the hurt silence. 'I'm sorry, Nelly,' she said, and clasped the child in a heartbreaking hug. 'It's almost as if he's still part of my body. But he will love you. I know he will.'

Eleanor nodded with the thought: on your terms, Louise, on your terms.

Louise and the baby were so tightly bound together that Eleanor was pushed to the margins of their relationship. A haze covered Louise's eyes, the pupils permanently dilated, as if she was stoned, lit only when her son suckled. Eleanor watched his mouth grip the elongated tit and imagined a sourish milk, until the cut of Louise's expression rebuked her voyeurism. Motherhood was draining Louise. Her rich hair had grown dull and her skin, like peeling varnish, disclosed a greyish tinge, her mother's northern cast underscoring her father's lustre. Eleanor was shaken to discover that Louise was a stranger.

She turned to look at herself and saw, as if for the first time, the redness of her hair, the whiteness of her skin and the moth wings flaring under her eyes. Louise's voice censured her appearance but when she turned around her friend was sleeping, head adrift on the pillow, mouth open. Homer was tucked beside her, the crinkles in his face rounded after his feed. She tried to picture him fully grown but decided that he was nicer as he was now. Instead, the dark shape of a haunted old woman at a window formed in her eye. She must move. Now was the time to go. At that thought the room lurched and the future gulfed before her.

Come December Eleanor was no longer the sole bread-winner in the roost. Louise had returned to the Café Aurore, taking shifts that alternated with Eleanor's working hours. Nights when the girls chafed to tear loose, Mireille bore the child to her quarters on a ripple of endearments.

'He'll be a perfect little European,' Louise claimed. 'An Irish-Greek who speaks English and French.'

'Better than the other way around. But Greece isn't in the EEC.'

'Not yet, but when it sees the Irish getting rich and fat it'll want to join.'

'Are you going back?' Eleanor blurted the question which had been niggling her for some time.

Louise dug her hands into her pockets and after a long silence said, 'I don't know. What about you?'

Eleanor shook her head. 'No. Whenever I think about it I feel a trap closing on my heart.'

'I know this sounds stupid, but I'd like to show Homer off to the parents. Although Mother wouldn't know which end was up.'

'She had two of her own.'

'Blips on the screen, my dear. She'd make a big fuss as long as he didn't puke on her. Leo would be potty about him.'

'Sounds like you're packing your bags already.'

'Not really. Then I think, what would I do? I'm not pushed about going back to college.'

'Marry a farmer and get rich and fat.'

'Ha! Five pairs of wellies in the hall.'

'And lashings of spuds for the dinner. But seriously, where do you think we'll be at the end of the century?'

Louise shook her head. 'I don't know. We'll be menopausal – if we're still around.'

'Alive but dying.'

'I'd like to have a rake of kids by then. And a nice house and a nice man.'

The trap tightened slowly over Eleanor's ribs. 'I couldn't do that.'

'Don't be so negative, or you'll end up a nun.'

'Sure.' Eleanor refused to share the image of madness that hung before her like a face in a mirror.

'We'll all be talking the one language.'

'Or using thought transference.'

'And what about our voices?'

'We can sing.'

'Not you.'

To prove her friend wrong, Eleanor began to climb the stairway to heaven. Louise, taking the tune, linked her friend's arm and they sauntered in song down the street. Their gaiety waned on entering the bar. A forlorn hush numbed the air. No radio played. The pinball machine was silent, its streaming lights offending the semi-dark.

'*Salut*, Eleanor.' Alexandre rose from a circle of glum faces at the back of the room. His greeting kisses were pressed with a consolatory solemnity.

'What's up?' Eleanor scanned the sombre group.

'Didn't you hear?' A pug-faced boy scowled at her.

Alexandre patted her shoulder. 'John Lennon was shot today.'

The improbability of the deed smote Eleanor, as though murder was extraordinary. 'Why?' She gaped. 'Who would do that?'

The mourning heads swung like bells.

'Crazy.' Alexandre put a finger to his head.

'He was a Messiah,' the puggish one said.

'Didier is right,' said another.

Louise blinked quickly against the cigarette smoke. 'I liked that song "Jealous Guy".'

Beside her, Didier sang the chorus, his accent bending the words. An accompanying hum droned around the table.

'My mates are in a band,' Alexandre explained to Eleanor. 'Concorde.'

The boys continued to hum.

'No, he wasn't a Messiah,' Eleanor said suddenly.

'Listen, baby' – Didier put a sneer on the English word – 'do you know "Imagine"?'

'Yes. It's a nice song. But it's a cliché,' she replied. 'Messiahs speak quietly.'

'So that no one can hear them.' The boy mouthed facetious nothings to his band.

'So that the people who listen are the ones who most want to hear.' She overrode his mockery. 'And they lead by example.'

'. . . staying at the Amsterdam Hilton . . .' quavered a voice across the table.

The rest of Concorde throttled into the refrain.

'The Hilton!' Eleanor scoffed. 'He'd have done better to buy the chambermaids a champagne breakfast.'

'Yes,' Alexandre cheered, 'and the commis – but not the chef. Above all, not the chef.'

Louise interrupted his chant. 'Well at least he was a house-husband.'

'His one mistake,' Didier complained.

'Why?'

'It killed his music,' said the boy facing her.

'The woman is for the hearth,' declared Didier.

'Dream on,' Eleanor chided.

'She is made to bear children.' The boy's tone was fierce. 'The home is a womb.'

Louise laughed. 'And what are we to do: sit around all day waiting for your little seeds to sprout?'

Eleanor joined her friend's laughter.

'No.' Didier seized Louise's hand in a burst of fervour. 'Woman is passive and restful. Man is active. He needs to burn out his energy in the world.'

'I still think she needs to get out of the house.' Louise turned coy.

Eleanor swallowed the last of her beer and stood up. 'I've had enough.' She addressed Louise in English: 'Are you coming?'

Pursing her lips, Louise glanced at the group. 'I'll stay for a little bit.'

Outside, Eleanor shuddered in the chill of a foot-step on her grave. The tinkling rain of glass which had held off for so long broke in her again. Had she the courage to keep on walking through it until she emerged alone on the other side?

For all his fine talk, Didier was a home-wrecker. While Eleanor stayed to watch the sleeping child, Louise was out listening to Concorde break the sound barrier.

'But for you,' Eleanor murmured over the scrolled dreaming ear, 'I would jump ship.'

That thought recurred when Louise did not show up until noon one day.

'Nice of you to stop by,' Eleanor said.

Louise sat with elbows planted on the table and pressed her head into her hands. 'Give me a break.'

'What about *your* son? What about *me*?'

'I'm sorry.' Louise did not raise her head. 'Didier and the band are going on tour.' Fat tears dropped onto the table.

'I don't care,' Eleanor tossed from the door. 'Next time I may not be around to hold the baby.'

The following Sunday Louise humoured Eleanor with a picnic on the river bank.

'Homer thought you needed some fresh air,' she laughed.

'He was right.' Eleanor lay back on the grass, blowing smoke rings into the hazy sky. The water slid by endlessly. 'Did you ever try to feel the earth moving?'

'Well, I have felt it move once or twice.'

'Not that way. I mean like this here. Being still.'

'But you can't be absolutely still. Your body is always twitching.'

'Sometimes I want to stop feeling my body.'

'Then you'd be dead.' Louise tickled Eleanor's neck with a blade of grass.

Eleanor bunched her shoulders pleasurably. 'It's as if life gets too big and wants to fly out of your pores.'

'You should have a baby,' Louise said. 'Everything seems to be sucked out by an enormous hoover,' she reflected. 'Being a mother takes away some of your identity, too.'

'Imagine if there were no sexes.'

'Life wouldn't be worth living,' Louise guffawed.

'I suppose not.'

'Look at Homer's little dickie, it's cute.'

'As long as he keeps it out of trouble.' Eleanor smiled at the child, whose tentative answering smile overthrew her. She brought him close, pressing her cheek to his. 'All of him is cute.'

'You can put manners on it,' Louise yawned.

They gave themselves over again to the balmy air and the mild anticipation of spring.

'I've been thinking,' said Eleanor after a while, 'it's time to cut out of here.'

Louise sat up. 'Not home?'

'No. On.' Eleanor slid her arm along the ground. 'The earth has stopped rolling. And I'm fed up ironing lingerie.'

'At least you get to eat the chocs.'

'Not any more. Ever since M. Riche came back there's been a big black cloud in the house. Now it's her I feel sorry for.'

'Where will we go?'

'To the light. To the light.' Eleanor jumped to her feet and slowly twirled, taking in the comfortable panorama of bedded plains blueing to a rippled horizon, until her eyes met the yellow walls cresting the fields. 'It's over,' she said. 'The town has vanished and all that's left is a heap of stones.'

'Eureka!' Louise bounded up beside Eleanor, hauling the baby onto her hip. 'We'll go to Greece – to Dad's dreamspace.'

'And we'll live on honey and wild thyme!'

'We'll bring Mme Riche and Mireille!'

'And all the banished children.'

And they were dancing ring-a-rosies, their abandon pealing in the lucent dusk.

Eleanor's fingers fleshed the rain-scored grooves of a kouroi buttock. The marble was smooth and her fingers reached through it to the snow-white angels of the stonemason's yard and to the rough stone which had anchored her childhood. The stillness of the museum was a qualified echo of the stopped time in the cemetery, the suspended hush of a hiatus that answered Eleanor's mood.

Since her arrival in Athens eight months ago, she chafed to leave, her feet tingling with the need to move. But Louise stuck her heels in and put up a hundred arguments against leaving: 'We need money – I'm not exactly sure where the dreamspace is – anyway, what the fuck would we do out there with no man? Shag the sheep?'

Between them, Homer stood, his wide face wincing and flinching at every shift in their tone. His innocence accused them. Already Eleanor could see traces of Ronan in these fidgets and in the hair which had promised so dark but was now lightening to an incongruous flax, so that strangers were not sure which of the girls was the child's mother. They had allowed him to become a stray puppy, wandering from table to table in the hostel canteen, accepting scraps. Most nights he shared Louise's sleeping bag but sometimes he snuggled in beside Eleanor, his body soldered to hers by the clammy heat.

Louise, remembering a distant cousin who ran a photo shop in Piraeus, had got a job there, while Eleanor gave English-language tours of the infrequently visited museum, where she felt comfortable. Tourists preferred to trip over the broken stones on the Acropolis. The statues, with knee bent, shoulder tilted, foot pointed for the next step, were cold bodies waiting to be reinvested by the gods. As a light from a high, barred window fluttered over the corner of a chiton, she wondered what it would take to start them up. She saw them bounding along the streets, larger than dreams, scattering the tawdry shelters of concrete and glass. The air they breathed made her giddy. No wonder they had been locked up. The glare and pressure on those streets startled Eleanor every time she stepped out of the museum. Here she drew looks as never at home, where the only object of interest was her misshapen arm. Louise's glamour, in turn, was diluted by the throng of features so like her own, casting Eleanor's lightness into relief.

In the queue for the hostel shower that evening, Eleanor felt light-headed. Was it something she ate – or hadn't? They were subsisting on rice, retsina, yoghurt and feta. On Sundays they went out to drink coffee with a curl of lemon on the side and to eat a sweet pastry. Sitting on the floor, Eleanor rested her back against the wall. The queue was longer than usual tonight; the high-summer travellers were moving in. Most, like her, sat listlessly silent, ignoring a sharp American voice bewailing capitalism on the kibbutzim.

Framed by the partly opened door of the canteen were Louise and Homer. They sat at one of the formica tables that so reminded Eleanor of school. The boy's eyes engaged hers for a moment, then, affronted, he turned towards his mother's chest, as if hunting for the milk that had dried more than a year ago. Louise accepted a light from a disembodied hand and chatted to the person outside the frame. Homer blurred for a moment to Aoife's infant shape, his Aunt Pixie rising now toward adulthood. A familiar estranging coldness swept Eleanor. She was disquieted by the sense that she was watching a film of her own life running away from her. Someone tested a guitar. Random chords struck, then faded, with no tune to carry them. The past sent up bubbles of memory to burst on the surface of her mind. Her father played the guitar. His song book was there in the suitcase whose puckered pink lining still held grains of honeymoon sand. But the suitcase was gone. The escape hatch. She should have buried it. She saw Ray's birds, again, on the idle sea. No ambition. No baggage. Soon, Eleanor thought, she would be older than her parents were when they died. She thought of them now as strayed children.

Homer slept sound as a stone in Louise's arms. The

hand poured her a glass of beer, which she sipped between pulls on her cigarette, gestures so familiar that Eleanor could see them with her eyes shut. She recalled slipping into Louise's body and long before that her need to be lit by her flashing beauty. They had become Derby and Joan, ingrained in one another's lives, too lazy to part. Eleanor swayed as she stood to go into the shower. Something was breaking inside her.

The cubicle smelt of apple shampoo. An auk's nest of hair encircled the drain. Eleanor stripped, and before turning on the shower, sat on the bench, grateful for five minutes' solitude. Looking at her dust-furred skin, she wondered would it ever be clean again. She opened her money belt and prised out Ray's last letter, which contained another, from Angela, written to mark Eleanor's coming of age. The domestic events dotted and crossed by Angela came from another planet: Ronan designing banks; Dermot dreaming of retirement; Mrs Tighe bedridden; Katherine dead, burnt ashes . . .; Tom in Saudi Arabia. But strangest of all was the message held till the end that, having 'reached her majority', she was to receive her inheritance. Her grandmother's post-office book now bulged with five thousand pounds. Eleanor read the paragraph three times. Five thousand pounds. What was she to do with this bounty? Her mind blurred and she laughed at the notion of herself as an heiress; then sobered. There it was, suddenly: twenty-one, the trap door. She hesitated, now, to cross the threshold, carrying her own life in her own hands.

The past crowded the cubicle, pressing her into a

sweat. She slammed her head against the wall scarred by the curses and moans of other travellers. ÇA ME FAIT CHIER . . . *Dermot so hurt* . . . NO A LA GUERRA CIVIL . . . *we love you still* . . . JESUS SHAVES UNDER HIS ARMS . . . *your home* . . . KILROY WAS HERE . . . *can't lock out people who love you* . . . HASTA BANANA . . . *for ever. . .* Hands swarmed over her. She tried to shake them off but they came on, plucking at her skin, tearing her limbs, stealing her body. No, she wanted to cry, but they had taken her voice.

Eleanor woke surrounded by whiteness. She twisted her head to the window's slice of blue. Shutting her eyes, she remembered snow and the swish of her arms and legs making an angel. She wanted to rest for ever in this stillness, but slowly, rustling noises and groans impinged on her. A hand raked back the screen beside her bed and when the nurse reached to lift the bedclothes, Eleanor shook in delirious chill. Seeing the nurse's broad hand approach her forehead, she shrank away, digging herself into the bedclothes. The nurse gave up and from her refuge Eleanor heard the screen jangle to.

Only the fire of Eleanor's hair was visible on her pillow in the high afternoon sun.

'Jesus, Nelly, you look like a ghost.' Louise deposited a bunch of dusty grapes on her bedside locker.

Homer stood wide-eyed, staring up at the steel bed.

'I died.'

'Don't be stupid. You had a burst appendix.'

The flame wavered on the pillow. 'I died, Louise. I was dismembered.'

'Nelly, you collapsed with a burst appendix. *And* you were robbed.'

'That's a laugh.'

'I don't see why. They took your money belt. That means you've no passport, no dosh – no nothing.'

Eleanor grinned.

'I went to the embassy but ...' A puzzled expression crossed Louise's face. 'You really don't care.'

'No.' Eleanor watched Homer's grimy hand reach for the grapes. His eyes at the last moment flicked to her. 'Go on,' she said. 'I can't eat.'

'Do you feel awful?'

Eleanor's mouth smacked drily. 'Not awful. Just weird.' Nameless, numberless days slotted in and out of the window. Needles stabbed her wasted buttock, bringing tears to her eyes. The daily bowls of rice pudding made her gag. A doctor came and, jumbling Greek and English, told her she would have to eat, have to walk.

'Can I have a cigarette?'

The doctor snorted. 'You kidding?'

Eleanor looked away to the window.

'It's not OK what you do.'

'What's that?'

'Kill yourself.'

A week later Eleanor's cubicle screen was wheeled away to seclude a mangled accident victim. Agony stretched before her. The pain which had seemed so intensely her own now spread the length of the corridor, which was as crowded as a railway station in rush hour. Mattresses were ranged on the floor between beds, nurses stepped over the sick to enter the wards. A group of pyjama-ed youths cheered when her screen was removed, for with her the only source of light in the room had been concealed. She wanted to apologise.

Later that evening when the visitors tumbled in, a short bulky woman left her husband's side and approached Eleanor's bed. Her fingers travelled faintly the length of the girl's cheek and jaw, and patted her streeling hair. It was not the touch of curiosity which she had expected for her outlandish whiteness and redness, but one of endearment. On subsequent evenings the woman flickered courteously at Eleanor but did not come near her until the afternoon of her husband's discharge. She helped the tubercular man into a baggy black jacket and grey trousers and wrapped a black shawl across his chest. Leaving him seated on his bed, she stepped over to Eleanor. She took the girl's weak hand in both of hers and held it a moment, stroking it. From her shopping bag she pulled out a jar of rose-petal jam, the Greek gesture of hospitality. 'One thousand petals,' she said. Eleanor could see them suspended in the blood-red jelly and she thought of foreskins culled from pretty youths. The woman must be a witch.

Eleanor smiled. 'Thank you. Thank you.'

The woman nodded and returned to her husband. Cradling his arm in hers, she guided him out of the ward.

EPHESUS — EPHESE

How's this for a fine broth of a girl?

This is the centre of wimmin power – Maia, Aphrodite, your old friend Holy Mary, Magdalene and now me!
Wish you were here?!
Ha! Ha! Good pickings on the beach.

Love
Louise and Homer

After all these years she still intertwined the LS of Louise and love. Eleanor turned the card over to study the goddess whose marble form was embellished with dozens of eggs, blooms and creeping things.

'Looks like the Easter fucking bunny,' she muttered. She ripped the card and scattered the pieces under the bed. Lifting the bedclothes, she peeled a strip of plaster off her belly and peeped at her wound.

Gently, her finger toyed with one of the stitches, stirring a queer ticklish sensation. If she pulled the stitch, would her stomach unravel and spill its shoal of organs over the sheets and onto the floor? She winced at the echo of pain in the wound's tenderness. Yet there had been no pain in the sensation of losing her body, only the panic of absolute liberty. Now she was empty. All that she had vomited in the days following her operation tasted of poison, culminating in a black stream carrying splinters of glass.

The operation had addled her hormones and the blood which had dried during the months of wandering returned. She lay in its hot pool, too exhausted to call for help. When the nurse found the stain she wadded Eleanor's crotch with a yard of cotton wool, like a nappy. Her body was lightening, even the numb drag of her crooked arm relaxed. These days in hospital were the first she had spent alone in almost two years. She tested the new space, then eased into it. Beyond her window she saw the traffic in the city tangle and untangle and the sky above the band of dusty sulphur shifted through daylight's blue and lavender. The low, continuous street noise abated only in the small hours. Far from that thrum, the hospital was sealed in its changeless fetor of bodies and panaceas.

Eleanor looked down the ward where the bodies propped and sprawled in the beds were whittled to grim resistance. Possibility dilated in her. She wanted to move out and touch the world again and find it new. She unscrewed the lid of the rose-petal jam jar and inhaled its fragrance. The scent hit her with the force of memory. This was the mysterious musk Louise had trailed when they first met. Her secret, the old woman's secret, now Eleanor's, too. Greedily she spooned the jelly into her mouth. The foreskin petals flittered into her stomach, lining it with innocence. She laughed.

Another emaciated man replaced the jam-giver's husband. That night Eleanor caught the nostalgic taint of nicotine drifting across the ward. Easing herself from the bed, one hand gripping the back of her hospital gown, she sidled to his bed to beg for a cigarette. His eye appraised her, then without speaking, he pulled the packet from under his pillow and offered it to her. She took one, smiling her thanks, and he tendered a flame from a lighter with 'I love NY' printed on its side. Eleanor pointed to the lighter, asking the man had he visited NY? He laughed, baring a set of irregular blackened teeth. He was a ferryman: people left things behind on the boat. She smiled at him and returned to her bed, where she pulled long and deep on her first cigarette in three weeks.

She befriended the old man and his sons, who kept her supplied with cigarettes, although she could not pay them until Louise showed up again. Louise was spending the money she had saved for the dream-space: 'Got a raise and I'm saving on hostel charges,' she tossed at Eleanor's objections. The day Eleanor was taken to hospital Louise checked out of the hostel and moved in with her cousin Andreas and his girl-friend. There had been no mention of Eleanor joining them there after her discharge.

Probably, the dreamspace didn't exist. That was the way of Louise. Besides, she thought, you can't live in someone else's dream. She coughed as the narcotic smoke hit her lungs. Forget the dreams. She crushed the cigarette and shut her eyes. Her hand played in the darkness. Her grandmother was speaking to her. 'I re-learnt the world. I found my way through it again.' She would go. Step out. Herself, clear, alone.

One thing she had learnt from Louise was how to cover her own ass. She had not yet told her friend about the inheritance. Now she forced her mind to focus on it, seeing it as a trove, luminous with the old woman's spirit. What dreams had she invested there? A good granddaughter would use the money in a way that might please her. Eleanor closed her eyes, part of her wishing it away. If the dreamspace didn't exist, she could make one. Slowly she built the picture of a house on a hill, with people drifting in and out, a rest-ing place for fugitives and transients.

At visiting time that night Eleanor crossed to the ferryman's bed. She handed her watch to his son in payment for the cigarettes. He tried to decline but she insisted and took the two packets he had brought for her. Back in bed she opened them and carefully shredded every cigarette, forming a nest of tobacco in her lap.

Homer approached the bed, and clambering over the hump of her legs, clung to her neck. Louise shimmered after him inviting the striptease stare of every man in the ward, and Eleanor's heart stopped, as it had when Louise broke on her world. She smiled at herself. Still a sucker for sex appeal.

'Hi kiddo,' Louise sat on the bed. 'When are you being released?'

'Next week.'

'Oh. Then there's something I'd better tell you. I wasn't alone in Turkey . . . I mean . . . Didier was there too.'

'What a coincidence – or was it?'

'Yes . . . I mean no . . . he would have come sooner but he was finishing a recording.'

Eleanor nodded sagely. 'At last the penny is dropping. We were cooling our fannies here, waiting for Diddums.'

'Well, I'm going to marry him.'

Homer's weight shifted against Eleanor's chest. She

ceased stroking his back, and looking down, saw that the round dark-eyed face was wobbling into tears. She tightened her arm around him, fearing the love his return had kick-started in her.

'I tell you, Nelly, love is incredible.'

'Gosh. Strange no one ever wrote a song about it.'

'Don't be so bitter.'

Eleanor groaned. 'This is giving me a relapse.'

'Well, Nelly, this is real life. Something you know nothing about.' She fumbled in her bag and drew out a string of seed pearls dainty as a baby's teeth. 'We bought these for you in the bazaar.'

'They're beautiful. Too nice for me,' Eleanor said.

'Oh, shut up. Let me put them on for you.'

Eleanor craned forward, glowing at Louise's touch. 'Thank you, you and Didier,' she said. 'So tell me the wedding plans. Am I best woman?'

'No, I am. We're going back to Paris and – well, this is where you come in.' Louise took a deep breath. 'Would you like to be Homer's nanny? We'd pay your keep.'

Eleanor closed her eyes. 'No.'

'I thought you loved him.'

'I do. But I don't love you.'

Silence strained between them, then snapped. 'I never asked you to.'

'You demand adoration from everyone.'

'Your problem, Nelly, is you don't know how to love. You depend on other people. You're sick.' Louise turned to beckon Homer.

Eleanor fiddled with the chain on the string of pearls.

'Keep them. They're only imitation, anyway.'
'That fits.'

Later, the nurse slipped the pearls off Eleanor's neck
and fondled them enviously. Eleanor shook her head,
indicating that they were fake. But the nurse continued to admire them.

'Keep them,' Eleanor said and folded the nurse's
fingers around the beads.

When the nurse was gone she rolled over and
stared at the uplit evening sky. The ward fell quiet,
suspended in the snooze of dusk. Eleanor pulled her
stinking clothes from her locker and prepared to go.

BEELINE
COMPETITION

Win the chance to become a Beeline author!

Beeline is an exciting new popular fiction imprint from
Blackstaff Press presenting entertaining and original books of
broad general appeal.

We are looking for new authors for future Beeline books – why not
enter our Beeline competition? The winning script will be published
by Beeline, and will be edited, designed, printed and marketed by our
award-winning team. The winner will also be offered a professional
author's contract with Blackstaff Press.

Submitted novels can be in any genre – romantic, historical,
detective, thriller etc – but must be original (i.e. previously
unpublished), well-plotted, with strong characterisation and
above all a lively, readable style.

Your complete typescript should be submitted on A4 paper, double-
spaced, and should be available on disk if required. Please enclose a
short covering letter (make sure you include your address etc!), a
one-page synopsis of your novel and a brief CV including details
of any previously published work. Send everything to:

BEELINE COMPETITION
BLACKSTAFF PRESS
WILDFLOWER WAY, APOLLO ROAD
BELFAST BT12 6TA

(If you wish your material to be returned, please enclose sufficient postage).

The closing date for submissions for the Beeline competition is
31 December 2002. Details of the winning entry will be announced
by 30th April 2003.

The judges' decision will be final. No correspondence will be entered into. In the event of
none of the entries being of a publishable standard, the most promising writer will be
offered advice on script development by an experienced Blackstaff editor.

Good luck!